"Why are you so eager to leave?" he asked, his voice low.

He seemed too close suddenly. It was impossible to ignore the vibrations between them, the flutterings of her heart and the tingling of her b_____ ___ ___ _____ *away from you,* she answere_____

"I...I don't lik_____ _____ _____ _____ _____ ur hospitality."

"Is that what it is?" He looked into her eyes, his gaze dark and unreadable.

She said nothing, fighting the soft humming of arousal, knowing it was useless.

He reached out and gently twirled a curl by her ear. She took a step back, resting a hand on the wall to steady herself. "Please, don't do that."

He slipped his hand in his pocket and leaned a hip against the wall. He observed her for a long, silent moment, the air electric between them.

"Charli," he said softly, "are you afraid of what is happening between us?"

Ever since **Karen van der Zee** was a child growing up in Holland she wanted to do two things: write books and travel. She's been very lucky. Her American husband's work as a development economist has taken them to many exotic locations. They were married in Kenya, had their first daughter in Ghana, and their second in the United States. They spent two fascinating years in Indonesia. Since then they've added a son to the family as well, and lived for a number of years in Virginia before going on the move again. After spending over a year in the West Bank near Jerusalem, and three and a half years in Ghana (again), they are now living in Armenia—but not for good!

THE ITALIAN'S SEDUCTION

BY
KAREN VAN DER ZEE

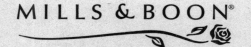

MILLS & BOON®

MILLS & BOON and MILLS & BOON with the Rose Device are registered trademarks of the publisher.

First published in Great Britain 2005
Harlequin Mills & Boon Limited,
Eton House, 18-24 Paradise Road, Richmond, Surrey TW9 1SR

© Karen van der Zee 2005

ISBN 0 263 84142 1

Set in Times Roman 10½ on 12 pt.
01-0405-50267

Printed and bound in Spain
by Litografia Rosés, S.A., Barcelona

CHAPTER ONE

HE WAS drop-dead gorgeous. Tall, dark and handsome. Charli smiled at the cliché, forgetting for a moment the burden of her troubles as she watched the man guiding the sailboat towards the dock.

Strong, square shoulders. A lean body that moved with confidence and grace. Thick black hair, sexily wind-blown and rakishly long. Yes, definitely, *very* good-looking. And, going by the fancy boat, probably plenty rich as well.

He might be exactly what she needed.

The August sun here on the Italian coast was still bright and hot in the late afternoon and Charli squinted a little to see him better. Thirtyish, she guessed. Dark glasses obscured his eyes. She watched as he tossed the line onto the dock, then lithely jumped from the boat to loop it expertly around the cleat, his tall body athletic and easy on the eyes. White shorts and a blue T-shirt showed off muscular legs and arms that were nicely tanned. She felt an annoying little thrill of feminine awareness at all that male splendor and tried to ignore it. This was not the time for romantic fantasies.

She was in trouble and she didn't care about how handsome he was, or how rich, or how fancy his boat. What mattered was that these attributes together probably spelled a certain sophistication that included a command of the English language. And, more than anything else right now, what she needed was someone who spoke English.

Alone in a foreign country, lost and clueless, Charli sat on a wooden bench in the marina, contemplating the fact that this was no way to start a new life. Or at least a New Chapter in her life. Being clueless was against all the rules on the list she had made for herself.

In this New Chapter of her life she was going to be on her own, all by her happy own self, and she was going to do exactly what she wanted to do when she wanted to do it. No one to answer to, no one to please, and no one's orders to follow.

The freedom was going to be glorious. And the best part of it—so she'd told herself—was that she was going to get started with this adventure in sunny Italy.

And now here she was, lost, helpless, clueless. Also sunglasses-less. They'd fallen as she'd struggled out of the train from Naples dragging her luggage. And then she'd stepped on them with a fatal crunch, almost losing her balance as she'd tried to side-step them. Not a good omen, if you wanted to think about it that way.

She did not want to think about it that way.

It had been just an accident, that was all. She'd buy herself a new pair tomorrow.

I told you it was a bad idea to go to Italy on your own. She could almost hear Rick's voice in her head. Very annoying. The Rick Chapter was over and there was no room for him in the New Chapter, which was definitively Rickless, and perhaps even reckless.

"You don't even speak the language," he'd said. "You don't know what that apartment looks like. It might be a rat-infested medieval dump! You're not being sensible, Charli!"

"It will be an adventure!" she'd said, not allowing herself to be scared off. She'd smiled bravely, fluffed her newly-cut short curls and offered him a careless sassy smile.

He had not been amused, and for days afterwards had pestered her with his objections and then practically ordered her not to go. *Ordered* her, mind you.

That was when she'd decided enough was enough and had told him their relationship was over. She couldn't stand his controlling, overbearing attitude any longer. That had been a month ago and it was the best decision she had ever made, even if it had scared her to death to turn her calm, comfortable life upside down.

`And here she was in sunny Italy and her adventure to live on her own was now truly starting, be it not in the most auspicious way. She'd felt so brave, so courageous, but now, feeling hot, tired and lost, it was hard to feel heroic.

She'd arrived at the train station two hours ago, had waited for an entire hour for Signor Bernardini to pick her up and take her to the apartment, and no one had come. Well, never mind Mr Bernardini, she'd thought, she'd find the place herself. She had the address, so how hard could it be? It was right here in the historic center of this small town, not far from the railroad station according to the map they'd sent her. Maybe he was waiting for her there. She'd spotted a car rental place across from the station and had got herself a small box on wheels, thrown her luggage in it and followed the directions she'd been given.

Forty-five minutes later she'd been a nervous wreck, clutching the steering wheel like a drowning person hoping she'd survive the traffic. She'd cruised down every tiny crowded medieval street in this warren of an ancient town, unable to locate the place, unable to find a parking space anywhere so she could get out and find someone to ask. Finally she'd ended up at the harbor where the marina parking lot was the only place she could find to park. Her legs had shaken as she stepped out of the car, and she'd felt more like a wimpy rag doll than a warrior princess. However, she'd now recuperated and felt calmer again. So she was lost. Not the end of the world, was it? This was not the Sahara desert or the Borneo jungle. This was the middle of civilization, a small town in Italy full of people and pasta. She would survive.

All she needed was a guide who could physically show her how to find the way to the apartment. A guide who spoke English.

And here, right in front of her was a Roman god in shorts who might just fit that bill. The god straightened, whipped off his sunglasses and rubbed the bridge of his regal nose, then raked his hand through his hair. Her heart skipped a beat. Really, he was too good-looking to be real.

She came to her feet and moved toward him and at the same time he turned slightly and caught sight of her. His brown gaze zapped right into hers and she felt a jolt of electricity, like lightning slashing through the sky. He stood perfectly still and her own feet stopped moving.

Her heart raced and she forgot what she had been going to say, oblivious to everything but those eyes, so full of darkly glimmering reflections, like polished stone. For a moment she felt oddly disoriented, unaware of her surroundings.

A second of frozen time.

Then she dragged in a deep breath and swallowed. It was so hot standing here in the sun. So very hot.

''Excuse me,'' she said, and heard the unfamiliar, husky tone of her voice. She cleared her throat. ''Do you speak English?''

He nodded. ''I do.''

"Oh, good." Relieved, she thrust the paper with the address at him. "I've been driving around for an hour and I can't locate this place. I wonder if you could help me."

He studied the letter the *notaio* had sent her. Over his shoulder, Charli caught sight of someone else jumping off the boat—a teenage girl, all arms and legs and long shiny hair.

The girl looked at her curiously. She was sixteen or seventeen, Charli guessed, very pretty, with dark hair, silvery-gray eyes and a slim body clad in shorts and a pink cropped top, showing a flat stomach. A small backpack hung carelessly from one shoulder. The girl glanced at the paper.

"*Cosè questa?*" she asked.

The man replied to her in Italian, then looked at Charli. "I think I know where this is, but showing is easier than telling. We'll take you. It's not far from here."

Such beautiful words! Such musical intonation! This was exactly what she had wanted, yet suddenly she felt uncertain. Uncertain about the man, the heat waves between them. What was wrong with her?

"I don't want to inconvenience you…I mean—"

"It's not a problem. It's only a five-minute walk."

His face showed nothing but calm control, but she sensed he was well aware of the sizzle of attraction between them.

She swallowed. "I have a car." She pointed at the parking lot.

"So do I," he said dryly. "It's best you leave it here for now. There may not be a place to park it nearby."

Well, she'd seen the streets in the historic center, and she had a pretty good idea that there wasn't.

She nodded. "All right."

He pointed at the marina building. "I need a few

minutes in there and then we'll be on our way.'' His Italian accent had a distinct British flavor.

''Thank you.''

He stalked off. Charli took in a restorative breath and smiled at the girl.

The girl smiled back. ''Are you American?'' she asked.

''Yes. I just arrived from Naples. Someone was supposed to meet me at the train station, but no one ever showed up.''

''And now you're lost.'' She seemed to find this amusing.

''Yes. Hopelessly. I drove around for ages, but with the streets being one-way I couldn't follow the directions. I think they're meant for walking, not driving.''

''Where are you from in America?''

''Philadelphia.''

''Really? My best friend Melissa is from Philadelphia!'' The girl stuck out her hand. ''I'm Valentina Castellini.'' She waved in the direction in which the man had disappeared. ''And that's Massimo, my brother.'' She made a face. ''I want to go to college in the States next year, with Melissa, but he wants me to go to England.''

''I'm Charli Olson. Your English is very good. Did you learn that in school?''

''Yes, and from my American and English friends. I'm in an international school in Rome. We do most of our work in English. Massimo says it's important to have an international education these days, because of globalization and all that.''

The man in question emerged from the building. He'd changed from shorts into freshly pressed chinos and Charli felt her pulse leap as his dark eyes studied her for a moment. She could not read his face.

"This way," he said, pointing toward the marina exit.

Valentina put a hand on his arm. "Massimo, her name is Charli and she's from Philadelphia!" she announced with a clear note of excitement.

"Really?" It sounded a bit cool. Although there was nothing cool about his dark eyes and his dark hair that lay tousled on his forehead. He extended his hand. "Massimo Castellini," he said politely.

"Charli Olson." She smiled at him nicely, trying not to melt when his strong brown hand grasped hers. This was too ridiculous for words. Never before had she felt such a strong reaction to a man. And it was the last thing she wanted right now.

"Are you visiting a friend?" Valentina asked as they walked into the street.

"No, I inherited an apartment from my grandmother. I'm coming to see it and maybe stay for a while."

They stopped at the curb of the street and waited for the light to change.

"Your grandmother lived here? You're *Italian*?" Valentina's eyes grew big. "You don't look Italian."

Charli laughed. Her blond, blue-eyed genes had a more Nordic origin.

Massimo Castellini frowned at his sister. "It's not polite to ask so many questions."

"Oh, I don't mind," Charli said. "My grandmother was American, but she inherited the apartment from her sister who married an Italian, but they never had any children. My grandmother left it to me when she died earlier this year. I have no idea what the place looks like. I didn't even know it existed."

They crossed the street, turned into a cobblestoned street so cluttered with parked cars, motorcycles and garbage cans they had to walk single file in order not to get run over.

"This leads to the Piazza di San Bonaventura," Massimo Castellini pointed out. "Remember that."

Oh, sure, she thought. Easy. But she looked around and tried to take notice of the shops they were passing—a flower shop, a *farmacia*, a small coffee shop with a few chairs and tables out on the sidewalk—red and white tablecloths, very cozy. The smell of espresso coffee spilled out into the street.

Paying attention to her surroundings served the purpose of keeping her eyes off the man in front of her. For female eyes he was a vision well worth looking at as he walked with his long-legged stride down the street. Charli decided it was safer to look at, say, vegetables.

The open vegetable market they passed had lots of them—colorful displays of tomatoes, zucchinis, herbs, peaches, grapes, plums and melons, even fresh fish, she saw in passing. It occurred to her that this might well be the place where she'd be buying her produce in the coming months, and the idea pleased her. She'd learn how to cook Italian food, eat the Italian way.

Massimo turned another corner and she followed his broad back with Valentina behind her. A motorcycle whizzed past at alarming speed, a young man driving, his girlfriend in jeans and high heels behind him with her head against his back and her arms around his waist.

The smell of pizza greeted her, coming from a small outdoor restaurant, and she felt suddenly ravenous. She hadn't eaten for hours. Another turn down a cobblestoned street so narrow no cars could possibly pass through, then through an arch into a courtyard.

"Here it is," Massimo said and Charli took in her surroundings.

Apartment balconies rose above, full of laundry drying in the sun. A cat asleep near one of the doors. A potted palm. A scene straight from a tourist brochure. Or a movie. Any moment now Sophia Loren would step out on one of the balconies and call down to them.

"That's the one," Massimo said, pointing at a green wooden door, ancient, the paint peeling. Several name plates and bells offered the identities of the inhabitants and he leaned forward to read. "Here it is. You have a key?"

"No." She wasn't feeling very bright. "I was hoping maybe somebody was waiting for me here. They were supposed to meet me at the station, but maybe…"

He rang the bell, but no one answered. He rang one of the other bells. No success there either.

From a top-floor balcony on the other side of the court-yard a loud female voice called out to them in Italian. Charli looked up, seeing not Sophia Loren but an old woman with blue curlers in her hair bringing in her laundry.

Massimo said something back and a rapid conversation ensued.

Charli hated feeling so helpless, understanding nothing. Standing there like an idiot in front of this decrepit door without a key. What had she been thinking? What would this man be thinking?

That she was a total nitwit, of course.

Well, she didn't care what he thought. She didn't care what anybody thought anymore, least of all a man.

"She says they've all gone out and there's no one at home," Valentina whispered, translating.

The woman must keep tabs on her courtyard neighbors' coming and going. Clutching the laundry to her chest, the old lady moved inside, and Massimo turned to Charli.

"You're out of luck, there's no one on any of the floors, and no way to get in. And it's Sunday, so I'm sure the *notaio*'s office is closed." He glanced down at the letter from the lawyer and frowned. Charli wondered why he was frowning.

She reached out and took the letter from him. "I'll find the office tomorrow and figure out what happened." She smiled with a confidence she didn't feel. "Thank you for showing me the way here. At least now I know where it is."

If she could ever find it again was another question. On foot, probably, but by car would be a problem. Why was this so complicated?

"Where are you staying?" Valentina asked.

"I'll find a hotel. I know there are several, because I checked." Charli smiled confidently. "I'll have to go back to get the car first." Surely hotels had places to park for their customers.

"You've booked a room?" Massimo Castellini asked.

He was too damn tall. Making her feel small. Okay, she was small. And out of her depth as well. She squared her shoulders, trying to look in control of the situation.

"No. I was thinking I'd see first if I could stay at the apartment, and if I couldn't for some reason, I'd find a hotel." Staying in the apartment would save money, which was a good thing. She didn't mind camping out for a bit if that was what it took. Nobody had lived in the apartment for almost a year and she had no idea what it looked like, or if it was liveable. But seeing this weathered door and the shabby balconies full of washing, she wasn't so sure anymore.

"No booking? Then you're out of luck again," he said dryly. "The hotels are full at this time of the year and especially now with the musical festival in town this week.''

"It was on television yesterday," Valentina said for validation.

Charli felt her heart sink. "Surely there's some place, somewhere? I'm not picky."

"The steps of the Duomo, the church," he said helpfully. "A Swedish couple camped out there last night."

"You can just stay with us," said Valentina, as if it were the simplest thing in the world to invite a total stranger off the street to stay in your house.

"Oh, no! I couldn't! It's—"

Valentina shrugged and threw up her hands. "Why not? It's not a problem, is it, Massimo? We've got lots of empty rooms."

"It's not a problem," he said graciously.

Oh, God, this was against all her rules. This was not supposed to be happening. She was supposed to stand on her own two feet and call the shots in this New Chapter of her life.

Charli stared at him. "You can't just...I mean, you don't even know me!"

Valentina rolled her eyes. "You don't look like you're going to steal the silver." She grinned. "Isn't that how you say that? Not that I'd care, you know. I don't care for the stupid silver. Come on, it will be fun, and you can help me with my English!"

It didn't sound as if she needed much help in that department at all.

"You're very nice, but really, I can't possibly—"

"Yes, you can," Massimo interrupted her, his tone brooking no denial. "There's no other place to go right now. Tomorrow you can go to the *notaio* and handle the situation.'' Without further ado he took her elbow and steered her toward the archway, out onto the street again.

And against all her new rules of independent living, of making her own decisions, Charli let him. The first crisis in the New Chapter of her life, and a man was taking charge of her again.

A stranger, no less.

A sexy Italian with dangerous glints in his eyes.

CHAPTER TWO

IT WAS like something out of a movie, this whole crazy situation. Picked off the street by a wealthy Italian, she was now here in this luxurious villa in a room with a view of the Mediterranean. A gorgeous room with its own bathroom, complete with a bidet. All elegant misty-green marble and shiny designer fixtures and thick lush towels in the palest jade-green. Even designer toiletries were available for the guest.

Charli tried to shake an odd sense of unreality. This was not as she had imagined it. Her life had been so ordinary, so safe, and now suddenly it was no longer ordinary, and no longer...safe? She felt off-balance and uncertain.

"Will you be okay?" Valentina asked, lounging against the doorjamb, apparently not eager to leave.

Charli glanced around, wondering if there might be a way she would not be physically comfortable in this spacious room with its lovely furnishings and huge luxurious bed with its silk cover. "This is wonderful. Thank you."

"My room is the one across the hall." Valentina pointed. "If you need anything, just knock."

"Thanks, I will."

"Oh, and dinner's at eight-thirty, on the terrace."

The girl departed and Charli stripped off her damp clothes and took a shower in the sumptuous bathroom. It had been a hot, exhausting day and it was heavenly to feel the water stream over her hot, sticky body. She took her time and felt her fatigue wash away, felt quite revived actually when she finally turned off the taps.

Her wet hair wrapped in a soft green towel and her body in another, she searched through her suitcases, wondering what to wear. She thought about Massimo, tried saying the name out loud, the way his sister had with the stress on the first syllable. *Mas*simo. She liked the sound of it. Strong and manly, yet very romantic.

''*Mas*simo,'' she said again, and in her mind she saw the handsome face, that athletic body in the sporty clothes. Despite his attitude of cool control, she'd seen the gleam of something else in his dark eyes.

She felt a little shiver go down her spine. Did the man have to be so disturbingly...male?

She didn't need this. She didn't want anything to do with men for a while. Yet there was no denying the electricity that had sparked between them. And she knew that Mr Italy, in spite of his polite manner, had been quite aware of it. He had said or done nothing to make her feel that way. He'd simply helped her by guiding her to the apartment and later he'd generously rescued her from sleeping on the steps of the Duomo by inviting her to stay the night at his villa. That was all.

She stared at the blue top in her hands and tossed it aside. A suitcase full of clothes, and still she wasn't sure what to wear. She couldn't believe what had happened to her. There'd been no way to refuse; Signor Castellini had simply taken charge, marched the three of them back to the marina parking lot and ordered her to follow him in her rental car, after first telling Valentina to ride with her in case she lost him in the narrow streets. Which, of course, she had done promptly.

She wiped away a drop of water trickling down her cheek. Okay, sure, she was happy she had a bed to sleep in, but she was disturbed by this situation, her lack of control, her need to be rescued by a man. It was an unbearable thought. She'd escaped the clutches of one control freak only to land right in the house of another.

Massimo Castellini knew how to take charge and had no qualms about doing so, that was obvious.

And she hadn't known what else to do but obey—more or less. She'd had no choice, had she? She took the towel off her head and rubbed her hair with more force than necessary, muttering curses under her breath.

Well, right now she had to get ready for dinner and see if she could rescue some of her pride and self-confidence. Somehow she had to present herself as more in control of herself and her destiny, give a confident impression.

She glanced at the mirror and sighed. She was cursed with those baby doll looks. Big blue eyes, looking all helpless and vulnerable. She was twenty-six and could pass for eighteen, certainly in jeans and a T-shirt. A few months ago she'd cut her long hair short, hoping it would give her a more mature look. She wasn't sure it had. Richard had been furious—Rick demanded to be called Richard, which was more sophisticated in his opinion. She often forgot, much to his displeasure.

It had been Richard's fury over her hair that had finally made her admit to herself that things were not as they should be between them. She'd been a coward for too long. Not that she hadn't been warned. Bree, her best friend, didn't like Rick—Richard, had always called him Control Freak Ricky, but Charli had been in denial. That was over now. The lights had gone on in her head and it was all very clear to her now. She let out a sigh and surveyed her appearance in the mirror. Now she had to get rid of the girlish look.

She needed makeup, for sure. And she should act more

sophisticated, with more confidence. And wear her skimpy emerald-green dress. She reached into her suitcase and fished it out. Holding it out in front of her, she glanced in the mirror again. Maybe it was a bit too skimpy for the occasion. Didn't want to give the man any wrong ideas.

Instead, she selected white dress pants and a black silk shirt. Then she worked on her face, applying more eye-shadow and more mascara than normal, and painting her lips a deep, shimmering red. As she examined herself in the mirror, Richard's disapproving face flashed through her mind. A groan of frustration escaped her. When were these flashbacks going to stop?

She could wear whatever she liked. Control Freak Ricky was history. His approval or disapproval of the clothes she wore, the length of her hair and the things she said no longer mattered.

And certainly Mr Castellini's opinion didn't matter.

Except she did *not* want to appear helpless and vulnerable, even though the truth was, of course, that she was quite helpless and vulnerable at this exact moment.

She straightened her shoulders. Well, it was only for one night. Surely she could manage for one night?

Massimo stood on the terrace and stared out over the town below, which was glittering like a jewel in the darkness. He loved coming here. He'd grown up in this house, in this town, and it brought back happy childhood memories. He enjoyed being here because it was relaxing and gave him a place away from the frenetic pace of his Rome existence.

But he did not feel relaxed now.

Damn Valentina for inviting that woman home with them! He deserved his peace and quiet. He'd listened to

Valentina's teenage chatter all bloody day on the boat and now here was this perky blonde who probably didn't have much for a brain going by the events of this afternoon. No key, no hotel reservation. He took a deep swallow of wine but it did nothing to calm his annoyance.

After a day on the water he'd hoped for a quiet evening at home, and now he was forced to entertain this sexy blonde, as if Valentina wasn't enough of a drain on his energies. This woman wasn't an insipid wallflower, easily ignored, or likely to ignore him, for that matter. Not many women did ignore him—a matter of record rather than of shallow male pride.

His cellphone rang. He fished it out of his pocket to find a woman on the line, as if to prove his point. Somehow they always knew where to find him.

"Hello, Elena," he said politely, feeling a bit guilty for not being more enthusiastic.

"Massimo," she sang, "the rumor goes you're back!"

"I've been back in the country for a week, yes." After a few days of organizing his work at the office in Rome, he'd collected Valentina from school and driven south to the Campania coast. Mimma had already opened up the house and he'd been more than ready for a little relaxation after his exhausting foreign travels. In the villa he could work from his comfortable home office and still have the opportunity to spend time with Valentina, as he did every year. Although Valentina spent most of the year at boarding school in Rome, this was her home too. There were many ways to keep a teenager entertained during the school holidays—interesting camps and foreign trips abounded but, with their parents gone, he thought it was important for her to feel there was a home to go to and family to spend time with her, to give her a sense of having roots.

"Haven't seen you for ages and ages," Elena said. "What Godforsaken corner of the globe did you honor with your presence this time?"

"India and Mozambique. Lots of gods. Not so forsaken."

"How exotic! I'd love to hear all about it. Let's have dinner tomorrow, shall we?"

Her interest was not faked, he knew. As an architect, Elena actually had some understanding of the restoration work his company was involved with, was interested in the projects they undertook renovating historic buildings the world over.

She was also interested in him as husband material and, since he was not inclined to be a husband, he'd been avoiding her.

Fortunately, her dinner invitation was easily declined.

"I'm not in Rome, Elena. Valentina is out of school for the summer and—"

"Oh, of course. You're at the villa. How is she?" Elena sounded polite. She was not really interested in how Valentina was, he was sure.

"*Bene*," he said. "We've been sailing. She's pretty good, actually."

"You're such a good brother, Massimo. I admire you."

The flattery annoyed him, and he made some casual response and terminated the conversation. He couldn't imagine what there was to admire about a man taking care of his little sister. It wasn't charity or duty, it was *natural* to do so. It was what he wanted to do, of course. It was his mission in life to get her well-educated, to teach her good moral values—honesty, loyalty, integrity. She might be the only virtuous woman outside the convents, but by God he was going to try. He loved Valentina and he wanted only the best for her. Not that she necessarily appreciated this, but then she was a teenager.

He'd been a teenager once himself, and he suddenly grinned at the memories. He'd driven his poor parents to distraction. Not such a nice boy he'd been.

He took another swallow of wine and stared out over the sparkling town and the sea beyond. Years ago he'd wondered at times if he'd be a good father, but it was a moot point now and the thought seldom occurred to him these days. For a moment Giulia's face flashed through his mind. Red hair, green eyes, a laughing mouth. The pain and anger of loss still stabbed him at times, but that too was dimming as the years passed. What wasn't dimming was his conviction that he would not marry again. He could not imagine living with another woman—loving, trusting, laughing, sharing his soul. Not again.

His mind produced a sun-filled image of a blue-eyed woman with shimmering blond curls, and a disturbing restlessness crept through his blood. Ridiculous!

The cool sea breeze whipped the hair over his forehead and impatiently he pushed it back with his hand.

I should not have brought her home, he thought for the umpteenth time.

Well, what the hell should he have done then? Dropped her off at her rental car near the marina and told her goodbye? Let her fend for herself when he knew damn well there wasn't a bed to be found in town?

And then, of course, Valentina had to open her mouth and invite her.

Charli Olson wasn't his responsibility, but there she was, all blue-eyed blond helplessness without a key.

And who did he think he was fooling? He finished his wine and grimaced at the moon above. He'd invited her because he'd *wanted* to invite her. All that very blue-eyed blond helplessness had gone straight to his miserable heart.

She hadn't wanted to accept, he'd seen the resistance in her expression—her pride doing battle with her common sense. He'd also seen the flash of panic in those big eyes and he had almost felt sorry for her. She'd accepted because she'd realized she'd had no alternative.

Well, it was only for one night. Tomorrow she'd get the key from the Bernardini office and sleep in her own place. Woman gone. Problem over.

Something niggled at him. He remembered looking at the letter she'd given him with the directions to the apartment. It had been a perfectly ordinary letter, but something about it had triggered a faint ripple of concern. He stared into his empty glass and frowned, but for the world of it he couldn't think why.

It looked like a movie set—the handsome man standing on the terrace overlooking the town with its sparkling lights and the sea beyond, a full moon above glimmering the water. He stood by the stone wall on the far end, glass in hand, wearing dark trousers and a white shirt, open at the neck, the sleeves rolled up. He looked as if he belonged in a movie with his dark good looks. Charli had the eerie feeling that she was somehow living a movie, or a dream. As if this wasn't quite real.

She was nervously aware of his eyes as he looked at her. It annoyed her that she was so self-conscious about it. Why couldn't she be cool and collected?

It would take time to get over the feeling that she was forever being judged and assessed. How could she have put up with it for two whole years? It was scary to think that she had been such a doormat for so long.

But not anymore. She was a free woman now. Free to do as she pleased, free to speak her mind.

So why was her pulse jumping?

"*Buona sera*," he said. "May I pour you a drink?"

"*Buona sera*," she repeated bravely. "A glass of white wine, please."

A movable cart full of bottles and bar necessities stood at the ready. A table was set for three, a candle in a cut-glass globe throwing intimate shadows over the gleaming cutlery and shimmering wineglasses. Several more candles were lit on a low table on the other side of the large terrace.

He held up a bottle, already open. "A local specialty," he said, giving the long musical name she couldn't understand, so she looked at the label to read it. Falanghina del Beneventano, it said.

He poured her a glass and handed it to her.

"Thank you." She took a sip. The wine was cool and refreshing with a fruity flavor.

He watched her, waiting for a response.

"I like it." Not the most sophisticated of responses, she was well aware.

"Good." Humor glinted in his eyes.

"Sorry, I'm not much of a wine expert. I don't know the lingo."

"'I like it' will do. You don't need lingo to enjoy it."

She thought of Richard, who had known all the lingo, who'd pored over books and magazines, analyzed wine labels and discussed wine with friends as if it were an issue of supreme importance, like human cloning, or cancer research.

She took another sip and glanced at the glittering panorama in front of her. "What a gorgeous view." She pointed in the distance. "What is that stone structure sitting on the edge of the rocks near the water? Some kind of watchtower?''

''Indeed. There are many of them along the coast here, some dating back as far as the ninth century. The Normans built a number of them too, to watch for various invaders and pirates and other unfriendly sorts.''

''The *Normans* were here?''

He gave a laugh. ''Everybody was here—Greeks, Etruscans, Romans, Saracens, Normans, Turks.'' He paused. ''Americans.''

It took a second. ''Oh, yes, of course. The Second World War.''

''They landed not far from here, farther down the coast.''

In the distance the sea sparkled in the moonlight. The scent of jasmine wafted around her.

''How is your room? You have everything you need?''

''Oh, it's wonderful. This is a beautiful house.''

''Yes. Unfortunately, we don't spend much time here.''

''You don't live here?''

''Only in the summer for a while, when Valentina is out of school. It used to be my parents' house. We both grew up here.''

''And where do you live now?''

''In Rome, but I travel often, and Valentina is at a boarding school. But I assume my talkative sister has already told you all this.''

''Not that you didn't live here. She said you travelled a lot. I must have missed the part where she said you lived in Rome.'' Valentina had chattered all the way to the villa. Their parents had died when she was ten and now big brother was taking care of her upbringing. She'd sounded a bit wistful, as if it wasn't all fun and games.

He took a drink and observed her. "What are you going to do with your grandmother's apartment—if I may ask?"

"I was thinking I'd stay for a while, a couple of months anyway." She'd have to be back home in the fall for her parents' thirtieth wedding anniversary, but until then she could stay. "I'd like to see what it's like here. I was thinking of fixing it up if it needed work and maybe rent it out as a vacation place later."

And, of course, she could sell it, but the idea of owning a place in Italy appealed to her. Her friends had all been enthusiastic, planning trips already.

"Can you be away that long?" he asked. "What about your family, your job?"

Well, she couldn't be luckier when it came to her job. "I'm a teacher and work for a distance-learning school, online. I teach English writing to foreign students all over the world. I can do it from anywhere as long as I have an internet connection. I brought my laptop."

He leaned back against the rock wall, crossing his legs at the ankles. "Interesting."

She gave a little laugh. "I think so. I learn a lot of things from the papers my students write. Did you know that in Bulgaria nodding your head up and down means *no* rather than *yes*, and vice versa?"

His mouth quirked as he shook his head. "Yes, I did know."

She laughed. "It must be really confusing."

Valentina came flouncing onto the terrace wearing a short little black skirt and a tight red top. "What is confusing?"

Massimo gave her a long disapproving look, generated by her clothes, Charli was sure, before answering her question. At which moment Mimma, the housekeeper, arrived with a platter of sliced melon and prosciutto ham and generous shavings of what looked like Parmesan cheese.

Valentina took off like a babbling creek, explaining the intricacies of the Italian dinner with its various courses and how the pasta would come next but it was only the *primo* and not the main dish so she shouldn't have too much of it because meat or fish would follow, but she, Valentina, didn't eat pasta usually, and—

"Why not?" Charli asked, stopping the flow of words. "What kind of Italian are you if you don't eat pasta?"

"Pasta makes you fat," Valentina declared with true teenage conviction. "Also, I don't drink coffee. Only green tea."

"Does coffee make you fat too?" Charli asked. She could not resist.

Valentina tilted her chin in defense. "Of course not. It's just bad for you."

"I see." Valentina's ideas were no doubt being influenced by her international friends at school. She only hoped she wasn't on some flaky diet. Charli was aware of Massimo calmly eating his melon and ham, apparently content not to join in this conversation.

The pasta arrived, in a delicious mussel sauce, and Valentina had a couple of spoonfuls of it because mussels were good for you, and then there was fish with tomatoes and herbs and after that marinated peaches for dessert.

Charli was infinitely grateful for Valentina's chatty presence. Being alone with Massimo would have been nerve-wracking. Just watching him eat was affecting her pulse-rate and her body was feeling tingly and restless. It was very disturbing. He said very little, letting his sister dominate the conversation, and Charli wondered what was going on in his head. If he knew how he made her feel…if he felt… She couldn't even think straight.

Valentina decided to pass on the dessert and excused herself to go inside to watch television and there she was, alone on a moonlit terrace with the sea beyond and a man who messed with her body chemistry.

Candles flickered and danced. The breeze stroked her skin, the air velvety soft and fragrant with jasmine. The peaches were sweet seduction on her tongue. Her blood ran warm with wine and wanting.

A scene straight from a romantic movie. She could see the possibilities in her mind. Another glass of wine, the moon above, the glittering sea. The man kissing the girl with all his seductive Italian charm. The girl practically swooning by the magic of the kiss.

Oh, lord, she had to get out of here.

She stood up. "I'd better go in as well." She managed to sound calm. "I've taken up enough of your time."

"Not at all. You must have a *digestivo* first. Sambucco, or some of Mimma's homemade *limoncello*, perhaps?"

She *must*? The word rang warning bells. *Oh, don't overreact*, a little voice said inside her head. She hesitated.

"Please, sit down," he said. "I'd enjoy some adult company. I admit that spending time with a teenager challenges my patience sometimes." He lifted a frosty bottle of *limoncello* Mimma had just brought to the table and she sat down again and nodded.

"I'd love to try that." Well, she would, *must* or not.

He poured them each a small glass of the icy-cold lemon liqueur and she sipped it, savoring the sweet lemony flavor.

"Good?" he asked.

"Very. Everything was delicious. A wonderful dinner." She took another sip. "And your sister is great— she's bright and fun. I enjoyed her."

"But she's only seventeen. And she's headstrong and not always realistic about what she wants."

"I'm sure it's not easy raising your teenage sister," she said, "but she's a nice kid, so you must have done something right."

He gave her a considering look. "I try, but I think my talents lie elsewhere."

In running a company and making lots of money, she assumed. Valentina had said her brother owned an international consulting business specializing in restoration projects.

"What kind of restoration projects?" she'd asked.

Valentina had waved her hand in a casual gesture. "Oh, ancient palaces and castles and all kinds of colonial or historic buildings." She'd grinned. "The world is full of ruins, you know, and some people find it important to preserve them."

"But you don't?"

Valentina had shrugged. "I like modern things. I'm sort of tired of old stuff."

Well, she was young. Charli looked at Massimo, who made money by fixing up the old stuff.

"Your talents lie in the business field, I expect."

He nodded, making a casual gesture with his hand to help along his affirmation.

"You have to deal with people and their individual temperaments in business too," she said.

His mouth quirked. "Yes, but if they're too much trouble I fire them, or sue them. Can't fire my own sister. Or sue her, for that matter."

"In the States you can try."

He laughed. It was a wonderful sound, deep and sexy. "An amazing place, that country of yours."

"I'm rather fond of it," she said, smiling. "Most of

the time, if not always.'' She finished the drink and came to her feet. "And now, if you'll excuse me?"

He stood as well, his dark gaze meeting hers. Her heart raced.

"I'll see you in the morning," he said, very proper, very polite. "Goodnight."

She swallowed. "How do I say that in Italian? Bonne...noche?"

"*Noche* is Spanish. It's *buona notte*."

"*Buona notte*," she repeated.

"*Bravo*." Amusement—and something else—in his eyes.

She tried not to rush as she moved her feet toward the door, but once she was inside she took a deep breath and realized how tense she had been. Knew too that he'd been aware of it.

"One night only," she muttered to herself as she got into the big, comfortable bed. "Tomorrow I'll get the key and be out of here."

In spite of her fatigue she slept restlessly, dreaming odd dreams in which Massimo featured in disturbing ways. It was light when she awoke, the sun shining and the birds twittering in the bushes outside her window. For a few minutes she lay very still, gathering her thoughts, realizing that today she would get the key to the apartment. Energized by excitement, she jumped out of bed and rushed into the glamorous bathroom to get ready for the day.

The house was very quiet, until she reached the kitchen where she found Mimma singing some schmaltzy love song, going by the word *amore*. She was washing greens at the sink.

"*Buon giorno*!" the woman said cheerfully, and then

went on to say something else. Charli gathered it meant something about eating breakfast and having *caffè*.

Coffee, yes, she'd love some coffee, and she smiled and nodded and Mimma fussed and brought food to the kitchen table. Croissants and honey and white cheese—ricotta, she realized—and an espresso coffee pot along with a pitcher of hot milk, so she could pour it the way she wanted. A lot of milk was what she wanted. The coffee was thick as syrup.

She wondered if Massimo was at home or had gone out.

"*Dov'è* Signor Castellini?" she asked. She'd learned about twenty words and phrases from her tourist book and she might as well try them out.

Mimma rolled her eyes. "*Studio,*" she said, pantomiming speaking on the phone and typing on a keyboard, "*due ora.*"

He'd been in the office for two hours already. A workaholic, maybe. Valentina had said that he worked from his home office here and was in touch with the headquarters in Rome and the project offices abroad on a daily or hourly basis. E-mail, phones and faxes made it all so easy.

She ate a crispy croissant, which Mimma called a *cornetti*, drank a cup of sweet, milky coffee, had some creamy fresh ricotta and a juicy peach, and figured breakfast didn't come any better than that.

It was too early yet to call the lawyer's office, so she took her guide book and sat on the terrace enjoying the cool breeze coming from the sea and read for an hour about the wonders of nature and the delights of the food.

Back in her room she took out the letter from the *notaio* and dialed the number. It took a while but finally a woman answered. But not one who spoke a single word of

English. She did, however, offer up what seemed a long speech in Italian of which Charli understood absolutely nothing. She asked where Signor Bernardini was. Another flood of Italian followed. No one else came to the phone to facilitate matters, which seemed odd. All correspondence had been done in good English, so surely somebody in the office had to be proficient enough to be called to the phone. Surely it must be apparent that she didn't understand and was not responding in Italian. Charli hung up in frustration. Fifteen minutes later she tried again and got a repeat performance from the same woman.

Now what? The only thing she could do was go in search of Massimo and ask for his help. She groaned. Why did she have to be so helpless?

Mimma pointed the way and moments later she knocked on the door and he called out telling her to come in.

It was a dream office. Large, light, super-sleek modern except for the jewel-colored oriental carpet on the marble floor that stood out in passionate contrast to the beautifully designed contemporary furnishings.

Massimo sat behind a desk, his eyes focused on her as she entered. He had on a striped shirt, but no tie or jacket. A lock of hair curled over his forehead. He held a black pen upright in his left hand as if ready to start tapping it on the desk at any minute.

She swallowed nervously under his regard, wondering what it was about him that made her feel so…insecure.

"*Buon giorno*," he said.

"I'm not so sure about that," she answered, and he quirked a brow.

"Already your morning is not good?"

She told him her tale of failure and he frowned. "Very

odd,'' he said. He reached for the phone and held out his hand for the letter. ''I'll give it a try.''

She handed him the letter, feeling like a child needing help.

''Sit down,'' he said as he punched in the number.

She obeyed like a good girl and watched him, listening to his voice. Italian was such a wonderful musical language. She really should try and learn to speak it a little, at least enough to not feel like a total incompetent.

Massimo frowned. She didn't understand what he said, but the expression on his face did nothing to comfort her. She felt a sudden flutter of apprehension.

Something was wrong.

CHAPTER THREE

MASSIMO put the phone down. "There's a problem," he stated, brushing his hair back from his forehead.

His words gave her no comfort either. "I could tell from your expression."

"Signor Bernardini had a massive heart attack on Saturday and is in hospital. His daughter is on her honeymoon on a cruise in the Far East, of all places, so the office is closed."

"His daughter?"

"She works with him. It's a family business. *Notaio* offices often are in Italy."

"Oh. And who was that you were speaking to?"

"The cleaning lady."

She swallowed, pushing back the sudden fear. "There is no one else in the office?"

He shook his head. "It's just a small father-daughter business."

She took a deep breath. "I suppose worrying about a key is rather shallow in the face of a heart attack and a ruined honeymoon."

"But understandable, considering you do not know the parties involved."

"Maybe." She hesitated. "Did the cleaning lady have any ideas as to what would be happening businesswise?"

"Her suggestion was to phone again later in the week." He tapped his fingers on an open file in front of him. "The daughter has been notified and hopefully she'll be back by then."

This was not good news. It was Monday now. She'd really wanted to get into her apartment today. Waiting around for several days was not in her plans. But she had no choice.

She came to her feet. "Okay. Well, thank you for making the call for me. I really appreciate your help, and thank you very much for your hospitality as well, of course. It was very nice of you to invite me to stay the night."

He arched a quizzical brow. "You are not thinking of leaving?"

"Yes, of course." She'd drive around and go down the coast to the next town and see if she could find a small hotel or a bed-and-breakfast place. In a few days she'd call the office again. In the meantime she could get an idea of the surroundings, relax, have a vacation.

Waste money. She had to watch her money. She felt a sudden surge of anger, remembering. How stupid could she have been to have had a shared bank account with Richard? And to break up with him just after he'd used the account to pay off a huge credit card bill—*his* credit card bill. He'd bought exercise equipment, having decided for both of them that it was important to have, that she should use it also, even though she'd said she hated exercising with machines. She was *not* going to exercise on machines. Not *ever*. Well, he'd said, she'd *better* use the equipment once they had it. It was good for her.

"Don't you tell me what's good for me," she'd snapped.

Okay, so her relationship with Richard had cost her on several fronts, but both her pride and her finances would survive.

Massimo observed her for a moment. "You are my guest and I cannot let you leave," he said then in a businesslike voice. "You must stay, of course. It's only a matter of a few days."

"I don't want to impose on you. Really, it's not necessary."

He raised an imperious brow. "Do I look like someone who allows himself to be imposed upon? I think not."

She tried not to be bothered by his tone, his take-charge attitude. Temptation took over, flavored with a hint of excitement. It would be so convenient to stay here in this magnificent villa, sleep in that beautiful bedroom, eat the wonderful food the singing Mimma prepared.

Be near this tall, dark and handsome Italian.

No, that had nothing to do with it. She was not, absolutely *not* interested in Massimo Castellini, whose dark eyes were still focused on her face, no doubt seeing her hesitation.

He leaned back in his chair. "Valentina will be delighted, naturally. She's bored without her friends. Where is she, by the way?"

"Still asleep, I think."

He glanced at his watch and shook his head. "She sleeps like no one else I've ever known."

"Teenagers need a lot of sleep. It's normal."

"Really?"

"Yes, really."

"Well then, I learned something today." He gave a half-smile. The phone rang.

She made a start for the door. "Sorry for disturbing you."

"Not to worry," he said, reaching for the phone. "And don't leave."

She gritted her teeth. Maybe he meant well, but his ordering her around hit a sensitive nerve.

"Is something wrong?" He must have seen her expression and she felt guilty, oddly, and then angry at herself for feeling that way. Man, she was a mess. He was only trying to be helpful, wasn't he?

"No, no. Thank you for your help." She rushed out the door like a naughty child and behind her his voice turned to sexy Italian music as he answered the phone.

In her room she stared blindly at her suitcase. Oh, damn, damn, she thought. Here I am, with a man in charge of my comfort.

Oh, don't be silly, said the voice of reason. It's only a few days. Surely, she could manage to live in a luxurious villa, sleep in a wonderful bed, eat delicious food for a few days? Really, now. It wasn't as if she were moving in with him, was it?

Massimo stood by the door to the living room and watched Charli and Valentina sitting on the sofa, looking through a fashion magazine. They were unaware of him, laughing, pointing things out to each other. One sleek dark head, one curly blond one—a nice contrast. He felt an odd prickle of annoyance as he noticed the easy way they communicated, heard their laughter. Charli was cheery and bright whenever he saw her with Valentina, or with Mimma in the kitchen, or the gardener in the garden.

With him she was very polite and tried to stay out of his way.

He didn't like it.

He didn't know why he didn't like it. He *wanted* to be left alone. It was often trouble enough keeping women at a distance, so he should be grateful she wasn't all over him and begging for his attention.

He wasn't grateful. He was irritated.

What the hell was wrong with him? He'd invited her to stay the rest of the week, this time without any prompt-

ing from Valentina. What had possessed him? She stirred
something in the hidden corners of his heart, something
he wasn't so happy feeling. He'd been aware of it the first
time he'd seen her in the marina and it should have been
a warning.

She'd been at the villa for several days now and the
studio di notaio was still closed. It might well be Monday
before the bride was back from her honeymoon in the Far
East and Alessandro Bernardini would be in hospital for
a while.

He'd felt a strange apprehension when he'd first seen
the letter Charli had shown him, and now he knew why.
This was a small town and last week he'd overheard a
passing comment that Alessandro was in hospital. There
were lots of Alessandros and he'd not made the immediate
connection, but at least now he understood his initial un-
ease.

He watched as Valentina shook her long hair loose and
Charli gathered it up and pulled it back from her face.
Her arms lifted, her breasts moving softly under the
T-shirt, a sliver of midriff became visible. Smooth, soft
skin. Nice full breasts.

His body reacted involuntarily and he gritted his teeth.
Well, he was a man, and this woman he'd invited into his
house was all feminine deliciousness with her soft curves
and bouncy curls. Not that she made a point of showing
herself off in front of him, as did many of the women he
came into contact with. Still, she was here in his house,
walking, talking sex appeal, whether she intended to be
or not.

The women in his life were usually not charmed by the
fact that he had a teenage sister who needed his love and
attention. Strangely, this woman seemed to be quite

charmed with Valentina while trying to keep *him* at a distance.

He watched as Charli studied Valentina's hair, then glanced down at the magazine, apparently studying hairstyles. Valentina looked happy and they were laughing, but he could not hear what they were discussing, and he felt unaccountably left out.

"Shouldn't you be writing that book report?" he asked Valentina in Italian, sounding rather harsh. They both glanced up at him in surprise and Charli let go of Valentina's hair. The happiness faded from his sister's face.

She snapped at him, saying she'd done it already and he didn't have to worry about her reading. She was quite capable of handling her summer assignments on her own.

He stalked out, went back into his office, feeling like a heel.

Thursday. The *studio di notaio* was still closed. Charli stared at the door, feeling helpless. She'd walked into town for the exercise and to see if by some miracle the real-estate lawyer's office had opened. The daughter had been expected to return today, but there was no sign of her. Charli felt a twinge of guilt. Surely the woman's first priority was her ailing father, not the work waiting for her at the office.

Charli had walked into town every day since the day after she'd arrived, when she'd returned the rental car. By now she had more or less figured out the center of the old town, which wasn't nearly so confusing now that she'd found some points of reference—her apartment with its flaking green door, and the Duomo, the old church from the eleventh century that dominated the center, the seafront promenade, and the *studio di notaio*.

The Castellini villa, with its graceful white arches and violet bougainvillea tumbling in glorious profusion over the walls that enclosed the garden, lay just outside the town, hugging a rocky hillside. The paved road for traffic circled around the hill, but for pedestrians a steep path, half stone stairs, half footpath, climbed up the hill and gave access to a number of luxurious villas hiding in the greenery. If nothing else, she'd have well-exercised leg and butt muscles by the time she finally got into her apartment.

So far she had made the best of the situation. She'd worked on her laptop, spent time with Valentina and edited her book report, teaching her the finer points of the English language, which were the only ones needing work. At least it made her feel she was giving something back. The villa's beautiful pool was certainly a plus, and she and Valentina would usually take a swim and lounge around for a couple of hours each day. She'd also spent time in the kitchen with Mimma learning to cook Italian dishes. The truth was that it was altogether a pretty good experience to be in the home of a real-life Italian family, eating the food and learning about things Italian.

However, regarding the man of the house, she was less sure she enjoyed her experience. Whenever they were together the atmosphere was charged with a sexual energy that wreaked havoc with her peace of mind. Massimo was definitely not good for her peace of mind. She did not want to think about it. Problem was she was thinking about it way too much. Thinking about *him* way too much.

Thinking about his wife.

"He was married, you know," Valentina had said a couple of days ago. "She died nine years ago in a car accident, the year before my parents died."

"That's terrible," Charli had said. "All this tragedy in such a short time."

"Yes." Valentina's voice had been soft. "Sometimes it doesn't seem like it's already that long ago."

"You must miss them a lot."

"I miss my parents. But I didn't see Giulia very often. They lived in Rome and I lived here. And I was only eight or nine at the time." Valentina stared into space. "She was very beautiful, I remember that."

Charli sighed, feeling not at all beautiful herself as she slogged up the stone path back to the villa, her body damp with perspiration. It was very hot and her sleeveless cotton top clung like a wet rag against her skin. She reached the gate, tired and out of breath from her climb.

Valentina and Massimo were in the garden, examining an exotic flowering plant in a large terracotta pot. Valentina was talking and Massimo laughed, put his arm around her and kissed her cheek with affection. He loved his sister, there was no doubt about that, even though she apparently drove him to distraction with her teenage behavior.

The big black wrought-iron gate creaked as she pushed it open and they looked up as she entered.

"Hi," she said, and Massimo's dark gaze met hers, held it for a moment. Her heart fluttered. Again. Her blood warmed. Again. Why couldn't she just keep this under control? So he was handsome and oozed sex appeal. So…all right, she was attracted to him. She might as well just admit it to herself. What woman wouldn't be? It would not be normal if he left her cold, would it?

But that didn't mean she had to give in to it. That was the main thing. Besides, it wasn't as if he was doing an all-out passionate seduction routine on her, trying to seduce her into his bed with his Latin charms. It was all much more insidious and subtle than that. More dangerous, because she had no way to fight it.

Massimo watched as Valentina grabbed Charli's hand and pulled her toward the house with her, saying she wanted to show her something. They disappeared inside.

His libido had been bored and unstirred lately. His work had taken him far and wide and he'd been unusually busy this last year. He simply hadn't had the inclination to spend his energy on women. But now the gods had handed him this sexy blond thing on a silver platter, so to speak. An obvious offer of temptation. And who was he to turn down an opportunity when it presented itself? She certainly stirred his fancy. Clearly, it was time for a little dallying. She was trying to avoid him, but it was clear she wasn't immune to him. Nor was he to her, and he might as well stop denying it.

"You have a boyfriend in America?" Valentina asked over dessert that night.

Massimo glowered at his sister. "Valentina!"

Charli gave an easy smile. "No, I don't. I just ended a two-year relationship."

"You did not have to answer," Massimo told her with a frown.

"I don't mind." She spooned up some ice cream. It was delicious, as had been everything else, including the wine. "Fortunately I am not heartbroken or on the verge of a nervous breakdown, so no harm done."

Valentina looked demurely down at her *gelato*, but Charli had the feeling she felt a sense of triumph over her older brother. Testing, testing. Well, if this was as bad as it got, he was a lucky man.

She finished her wine and Massimo refilled her glass

automatically. She'd already had quite a bit, but never mind. It was a very nice wine, in her humble opinion, and she was feeling relaxed and content, more relaxed than she'd been all week.

Her dessert finished—apparently ice cream didn't make you fat—Valentina went off to see something on TV, and Mimma brought two tiny cups of *caffè*.

Usually, after dinner on the terrace, Charli tried to escape soon after the espresso, except this evening something compelled her to accept the offer of a *digestivo*, and Mimma's delicious *limoncello* in its frosty bottle tempted her.

"Thank you," she said as she took the tiny glass Massimo handed her. She gave a sigh of contentment as she sipped the lemony sweetness. It felt so blissfully nice here on the terrace with the sea breeze stirring the balmy air, the scent of jasmine all around and her body warm and sated with good food and wine. She wanted to stay right here and enjoy the evening.

She did not want to listen to that little voice inside her, whispering words of warning. She took her glass and strolled to the stone wall and looked out over the town. It was easy to locate the lights of the Duomo, and somewhere nearby was the old *palazzo* that held her apartment. Parts of that building dated back to Norman times, she'd learned, remnants of an ancient fortification that had been rebuilt, restored and added on to at various times over many centuries.

Massimo came to stand next to her. She took another sip from the *limoncello*. "I'm beginning to recognize where things are," she said for something to say. "I can see the Duomo."

"Have you been inside yet?"

"Yes. It's amazing. So old, it's hard to believe it's still

there. My apartment building—it's to the right of there, isn't it?''

He took her empty glass from her hand and put it on the stone wall. ''Yes. You can't really see it, though.''

She sighed. ''I wish I could just get in.''

A moment of silence. She felt the tension in the air.

''Why are you so eager to leave?'' he asked, his voice low.

He seemed too close suddenly. It was impossible to ignore the vibrations between them, the flutterings of her heart and the tingling of her blood. *I need to get away from you,* she answered silently.

''I…er, I don't like to take advantage of your hospitality.''

''Is that what it is?'' He looked into her eyes, his gaze dark and unreadable.

She said nothing, fighting the soft humming of arousal, knowing it was useless.

He reached out and gently twirled a curl by her ear. She took a step back, resting a hand on the wall to steady herself. ''Please, don't do that.''

He slipped his hand in his pocket and leaned a hip against the wall. He observed her for a long, silent moment, the air electric between them.

''Charli,'' he said softly, ''are you afraid of what is happening between us?''

CHAPTER FOUR

MASSIMO'S softly spoken words were heavy with meaning. Charli felt her heart lurch with trepidation.

"Nothing is happening between us," she said quickly. Too quickly.

He placed a hand over hers and fire shot through her. She yanked it away. He laughed softly.

"Nothing at all?" His voice was deep and amused.

And then, before she had a chance to find a fitting answer, she felt his hands cradling her face and he was kissing her—a mere brushing of his lips over hers, teasing, tantalizing, but with a sensuality that melted away her strength and made her legs tremble. She should pull away, not allow him to just do this as if he had every right, but she stood there, incapable of moving.

A moment later he withdrew his mouth. "Was I wrong?" he asked softly. His hands still cradled her face and his dark gaze held hers. The truth hovered between them—he wasn't wrong, not wrong at all.

She stood rooted to the ground, her heart thudding against her ribs, and then he kissed her again. Not so softly this time, but with a passion that intoxicated her, made her forget everything. Everything but the feel of his mouth, the taste of him, the warmth of his body as he slipped his arms around her and held her against him. Clearly, under that cool, calm exterior, passion lurked, and she had no defense.

Her mouth opened to his and their tongues moved in a dance of desire. She leaned in to him, wanting more, feeling as if she was drowning in a sea of sensations. Feeling his body against her, warm and hard and wanting.

He released her and stepped back. Her knees nearly gave way and for a moment a pregnant silence throbbed between them.

''Forgive me my passionate Italian nature,'' he said, his tone oddly formal. He turned and stalked his way across the terrace back into the house.

She stood paralyzed, watching him disappear from her sight.

Sanity returned on a wave of fear. This was not what she wanted. She did not want to fall in love. Not now, not with this man who was altogether too domineering. She had the sudden urge to flee, run, race away from Massimo Castellini and his magical kisses.

It was hard enough to think she needed the help of this man to solve her housing problem. Now she had to do battle with sexual attraction as well.

She went inside, moving as if in a trance. Got ready for bed. Stared at the ceiling.

Images of Richard, at the beginning of their relationship. His charming grin. Memories of treasured moments. How deluded had she been? Then the painful end when denial fled and she'd seen the truth: she'd allowed Richard to walk all over her.

From somewhere came a wave of emotion—a mixture of pain and anger and regret. She curled up into a ball, closed her eyes, trying hard not to cry.

I'm going to do better next time, she thought. I'm going to be strong. I'm not going to fall in love with Massimo Castellini.

''Charli, this is unbelievably cool!'' Bree's voice rang bright and clear over Charli's newly acquired cellphone.

She'd found Charli's e-mails unsatisfactory, she'd said, and was calling to hear more details. "If I didn't know you better, I'd think you were making it up!"

Charli sat on her bed, yogi style, and grimaced, the phone pressed to her ear. "It's not cool, Bree. What am I going to do?"

"About what?"

"About Massimo. He's messing with my hormones, not to speak of my common sense." And here she was, Friday afternoon, and still not in her own apartment. Now she had a whole weekend to cope with. She closed her eyes. "I don't want to deal with all this stuff, Bree! I don't want to feel what I am feeling."

"What are you feeling?"

"Oh, God, do I have to explain that to you? I feel like a teenager when he walks in the room. I feel like I'm going to go up in flames when he touches me. It's like I have no control over my reactions!"

"It sounds deliciously passionate." Bree gave a sigh full of yearning.

"It's insanity! What am I going to do?"

"Excuse me if I sound simplistic, but how about doing what comes naturally?"

"Like *sleep* with him?"

"Sounds good to me. You never know what might develop."

"That's the thing, Bree! I don't want anything to develop! You, of all people should know how very much I do *not* want to be in another relationship right now. Free at last and you're having me sleep with an Italian more or less the moment I set foot on European soil."

"Who's talking about a relationship? The way to deal with a rich, glamorous Italian who has the hots for you is to have a glorious summer fling."

"I don't want a summer fling. I don't want any kind of fling."

Bree laughed. "And I think that it's *exactly* what you do need! Therapy, so to speak."

"Therapy?" Charli rolled her eyes.

"To heal the wounds that Control Freak Ricky inflicted on your soul."

Charli groaned. "The best therapy for that is not to get involved with a man again."

"Ever? You mean you're planning a life without a man in it?" Bree's tone did not hide her opinion on the matter and it wasn't good.

"For a while."

Bree gave a long-suffering sigh. "The good things always come to those who don't value them," she said theatrically. "You suppose if I came to visit I might be able to snare him? Does he like redheads?"

"His wife was a redhead." Valentina had shown her pictures of the gorgeous Giulia.

"Was?"

"She died. Nine years ago. His sister told me. And, as far as she knows, he hasn't had a serious long-term relationship since. She says he doesn't want to get married again."

"Mmm…well, maybe I change my mind about a fling with him."

"Why is that?"

"Men pining after a dead wife are a bore and you're forever being compared to this angel of perfection and of course you can never live up to expectations. On the other hand, knowing he isn't interested in marriage makes it easier to have a fling. Fewer possibilities for complications."

Charli made a face and with her index finger traced the

design of a peacock on the silk bedcover. She'd never had a fling in her life. Why waste time and emotion on something that was going to lead nowhere? Life was too short not to take love seriously. Maybe she was just old-fashioned, but there it was. She'd truly thought she'd been in love with Richard, which had turned out to be a mistake, but she had learned from it. Now she was just going to take a break from love and get her pride and confidence back in working order and *not* fall for the first Casanova who gave her smoldering looks and kissed her silly without her permission.

"I only want the real deal, you know that," she said, and Bree gave another one of her long-suffering sighs.

"I know, I know. Then again, who says this *Mas*simo isn't the real deal?"

Charli felt herself tense and poked at the eye of the silk peacock. "He's not. I *know* he's not."

You will have romantic moments, which you can enjoy in three beaches, where you can not only enjoy your time, but as well admire sun-set with the person of your love-interest.

Charli sighed as she read the assignment of one of her foreign students on her laptop screen. Not even in her work could she get away from love and romance. She'd felt on edge all day and Bree's phone call had not helped. She was irritable and had the constant urge to snap at somebody. But the only people around were Mimma and Valentina and snapping at them would not be cool, so she'd retreated to her room.

She was trying to do some work in an effort to find calm and composure before facing Massimo at dinner time, but the gods were against her. Out of cyberspace came this piece of writing about romantic moments and watching the sunset.

She dropped her head in her hands and moaned.

"I got an e-mail from Melissa today," Valentina announced as they sat down to dinner later that evening. "She's in Philadelphia and she visited the campus of the University of Pennsylvania with her parents and she really likes it." Charli heard the note of challenge in Valentina's voice.

Massimo carefully deboned the fish on his plate and didn't look up. "Is that so?" he said evenly.

"Yes. She's decided she'll go there next year." Valentina looked at Charli. "You said you went to university there. Do you think it's a good choice?"

"It was for me."

"Melissa says that—"

Valentina launched into an enthusiastic description, which was ignored by Massimo. Charli gritted her teeth. What was wrong with the man? Couldn't he see how important this was for his sister? Valentina had told her Massimo had decided she should go to university in England next year and she hadn't been able to convince him to change his mind, or to even give it another thought. By the look of it, he wasn't giving it much thought now either.

The girl's voice took on a pleading tone. She wanted to go to university in Philadelphia. Surely she could get a good education there! Massimo remained calm and unperturbed. Valentina became more and more agitated. She glanced over at Charli, her eyes begging for help.

"Were you allowed to have a choice? I mean, did your parents decide for you where you were going to study?"

Oh, no. Charli noticed the hardening of Massimo's features. Well, she wasn't going to lie.

"I discussed it with my parents, of course, but yes, I was allowed to make up my own mind."

"So they didn't think you were stupid and didn't know enough to make the right decision for your own life." Valentina's tone was caustic, clearly accusing her brother.

"No, they didn't. They believed it was important for me to make my own decisions." She couldn't help but add the last sentence, feeling Massimo's anger heating the air around them.

He shot his sister a warning look. "I know what you are doing, Valentina, and it's not going to work."

"Why can't I have something to say! Why do you have to make all the decisions about my education? It's a very good university and there's nothing wrong with me wanting to go there! It's a good university, isn't it, Charli?" she pleaded.

"One of the best in the US," she said truthfully.

Massimo's eyes were dark and dangerous. "That is not the issue. Arrangements have been made for you to attend university in England. I don't want you across the ocean and that is the final word."

"You never even gave me a choice! I should have something to say about it! It's my life!"

"The subject is closed, Valentina."

Charli could feel her temperature rise. His domineering attitude rubbed her the wrong way. Still, this was not her business and she shouldn't interfere. She bit her tongue, but it didn't help—she simply couldn't stay silent.

"I think kids should be taught how to make responsible decisions," she said, her good sense flying out into the night right along with her good manners. "If they don't learn how, who will do it for them when they're adults?"

"Yes!" Valentina cried out. "If you can't let me make decisions now, I—"

Massimo interrupted her, his jaw tight. Charli did not know what he was saying as he had switched to Italian, shutting her out. Intentionally, no doubt.

Face mutinous, Valentina stared down at her uneaten food, saying no more as her brother spoke.

Massimo stopped talking. He reached for his glass and finished his wine.

Valentina, close to tears, pushed her chair back and rushed indoors without saying a word.

Charli put her napkin on the table and stood up, ready to follow her in.

"I want a word with you," Massimo said. He picked up the wine bottle and refilled her glass.

Uneasily, Charli sat back down, feeling like a child about to be reprimanded. She hated the feeling and she clenched her hands in her lap.

"I understand you meant well," he said, "but I am responsible for Valentina and I have made certain decisions I will not change."

"About her education, her life."

"Yes."

Indignation flared again. "You mean she doesn't have any say herself about these matters?"

"I only want what is best for her." He came to his feet and looked down at her.

Warning bells. Danger signals. She felt herself begin to tremble. She was ready for all out battle. Yet this was not her battle. Massimo was her host. She had no business interfering in his personal business. It took an effort, but she managed to stay silent.

"You do not agree?"

She clenched her hands. "It doesn't matter whether I agree, does it? It's not my business."

"No," he said slowly, meeting her eyes. "Valentina is not your concern." There was a warning in his tone.

"But you are wrong." She could not resist. She *had* to say something.

He raised his brows. "Really?"

His haughty tone infuriated her. She did not like the way he was standing there looming over her. She stood up and glared at him. Even on her feet she still had to look up at him, but it was better than sitting down.

"Yes, really. No matter how pure your intentions, you should not make such important decisions without her input. You're much too controlling with her." So there, she'd said it.

He swirled the wine in his glass and studied her for a moment. "You are angry with me," he stated calmly, as if he were making nothing but a factual observation.

So she was. "I do not like controlling men." She was aware that her hands were clenched by her side. She tried to relax them, saw his gaze follow the movement of her fingers.

"But you're not angry with me because of Valentina, I think." His voice was softer now, full of suggestion. His words surprised her.

"I am not?"

"No." He took another drink and held her gaze over the rim of his glass. "I think," he said slowly, "that you're disturbed because of what happened between us last night."

Charli stared at him in disbelief. This had nothing to do with last night. She was angry because his authoritarian attitude toward his sister was infuriating, that was all. "That's ridiculous," she said.

"Is it? I kissed you and you liked it." He paused. "And you're angry because you didn't *want* to feel what you were feeling. Why?"

She glared at him. "You don't know what I was feeling!" She didn't like his presumptions, felt an instinctive defensiveness. Who was he to analyze her emotional state?

"I know when a woman's body responds to me." It was a simple statement, made without macho arrogance or conceit, which made the truth of it even more undeniable.

She opened her mouth. Closed it again. She couldn't think of a thing to say. Her thoughts floundered helplessly. What had happened here? They'd been talking about Valentina, and now suddenly they were discussing her reactions to him, Massimo. He was studying her with those dark eyes that made her feel he was looking straight into her heart. A wayward lock of hair curled carelessly over his forehead and in the night shadows he looked impossibly handsome in a pure sexual male way. She tried not to think of his kiss, tried really hard not to feel the warmth spreading through her at the mere memory of his hard body against hers, of the way she had melted into him.

He knew when a woman's body responded to him. Well, of course he did. She looked away, out over the sparkling town toward the dark sea. And he was right, she was angry and on edge because she didn't want to feel what she was feeling and she'd been fighting it all day.

"You've purposely been avoiding me since the day you arrived here," he said then. "Why?"

So he'd noticed. She shrugged. "Does that offend your ego?"

"I just wonder why."

He was altogether too calm and self-possessed. Where was his Latin hot-bloodedness? "It seems prudent under the circumstances," she said loftily, feeling rather proud of her rational answer.

"What circumstances? Are you afraid of the chemistry between us? Of what we're doing to each other?"

"I'm not doing anything to you!"

His mouth quirked. "Not intentionally, perhaps. But you are most certainly doing something to me."

Go take a cold shower, she was tempted to say, but managed to control herself. "Well, I'm sorry I—"

"And," he interrupted her, "*I* am doing something to *you*. Please, don't deny it."

"Denial is much underrated. It suits me just fine." Not the most intelligent of answers and she should know better. Her stint with denial in her relationship with Richard had not served her well. But right now she was not ready to admit to Massimo that he had a most disturbing effect on her. Then, of course, he already knew.

He studied her. "I like you, Charli."

She didn't know what to say to that. If only he'd said something like, *I want you, I ache for your body, I must have you,* or something equally dramatic and flowery she'd have an answer for him. But who could object to *I like you*? Not that she didn't know what he meant or what he wanted. He was simply too relentlessly courteous about it and she had little defense.

Like Richard, came the unbidden thought. He'd been so nice, so considerate in the beginning. She'd fallen at his feet like a wet noodle. She gave a little shiver.

Massimo put his empty glass on the table. "It's not a terrible thing, Charli. We are two adults. I'm sure we can handle it."

She could well imagine how he intended to "handle"

it and she had no intention of letting him. Not that it didn't have a certain appeal to fall in love with a sexy Italian, but it was not what she needed right now. He might stir all her female hormones, but he was all wrong. He was way too bossy. He liked too much to be in control. She'd been there, done that. Not ever again.

She took a step away from him. "I don't want to get involved. I don't want to handle any sort of affair. It would be a big mistake for both of us." She took another step toward the house. "I'm going to my room now. Goodnight." She turned and walked off calmly, trying to look dignified and not like a scared rabbit scurrying off to its hole.

Once inside her room she let out a long, nervous sigh. This was ridiculous. She had to get out of here, away from this man. Surely on Monday she'd get that blasted key? All she had to do was survive the weekend.

A couple of minutes later a knock came on the door and her heart leaped in her throat. Not Massimo, she pleaded silently. "Yes?" she called out.

"It's me, Valentina."

Charli opened the door and looked at the girl's worried face.

"Massimo was mad at you, wasn't he? Because of what you said."

"Don't worry about it."

"He's such a... I don't know the word. He always wants to boss me around. He doesn't think I know anything."

"He's responsible for you. He tries to do what he thinks is best." Well, that was true enough, she assumed.

Valentina gave a frustrated sigh. "But he *always* thinks he knows best! Like with his work. He's the boss, and he runs everything and what he says is law."

"And it looks like he's pretty successful at it." Which was an understatement.

"But I'm not a business project! I can think for myself, you know! I don't like to be...to be *managed*!"

Charli stared at Valentina, feeling her heart doing a little dance of sympathy. "I know what you mean."

"*Men*!" Valentina said with heartfelt teenage disgust. "They think women are stupid or something. Well, Italian men, anyway. They're so un-evolved! All they think we're good for is cooking and sex, in that order!"

Charli laughed. She couldn't help it. "Oh, come on, Valentina. If your brother felt that way he wouldn't find it necessary for you to get a university education, would he?"

Valentina made a face and shrugged.

"He'd go out and find you a 'suitable' husband and marry you off instead, like in the old days."

Valentina groaned. "Oh, puh-leeze!" She sounded so American it made Charli smile again.

"See? It could be worse. You could be planning a wedding."

Valentina gave a reluctant smile. "Yeah, well, I'm sorry if he's mad at you because of me."

"Don't worry about it. I can take care of myself. Go to sleep and forget about it."

"Okay. Goodnight, Charli."

"*Buona notte*." Charli watched as Valentina crossed the hall and disappeared into her room.

I've got to do something, she thought, something to help her stand up to Massimo. But what?

Once she'd moved into her own apartment, things would be easier. She'd figure out how to help Valentina.

* * *

A stack of papers. A bank account with lots of euros in it. Keys.

Keys!

They were like gold in her hand and Charli had a hard time not skipping along the cobblestoned Via Mercanti as she and Valentina made their way to the apartment. Finally!

It was late Monday morning and the call from the lawyer's office had come only an hour earlier.

"This is so exciting," said Valentina. "I can't wait to see the place. Maybe it's been remodeled and it's really nice. You never know sometimes with these old *palazzo* buildings. Inside they can be really cool!"

Charli smiled at the girl's enthusiasm. "It was owned by an old woman, Valentina, and it's been empty for a year. My only hope is that it's in good enough shape for me to stay in."

"Maybe it's full of antiques! Maybe there's a Botticelli painting nobody knows about! You'll be rich!"

Charli laughed. "We'll know in about three minutes."

They turned the corner and passed the little vegetable market. She knew the way exactly now, and she enjoyed a sense of competence as she made her daily walks through town, exploring little shops and hidden alleys and piazzas.

She had survived the weekend. She'd taken herself out of the house on Saturday, taking the bus-ferry to Positano and spending the day walking around and sightseeing right along with a million other tourists thronging the narrow streets. The place was beautiful, the busloads of tourists from all over Europe had been…well, overwhelming.

Back at the villa in the early evening, she'd found Massimo out for the evening and Valentina curled up in front of the TV. Mimma was off, so the two of them had decided to have dinner in town and then go to one of the outdoor concerts near the Duomo. They'd found a table at one of the many *trattorias* and ordered deep-fried calamari, a favorite of Valentina's. They'd followed it up with a pizza, finishing the meal with a bowl of *gelato*.

"I want to cut my hair," Valentina had said. "Short, like that." She'd pointed at a girl across the street who was being kissed in a most passionate way by a young guy in jeans and a black shirt. Everywhere in public couples were kissing and hugging with happy abandon, Charli had noticed. On park benches, standing in doorways, sitting on sidewalk cafés, strolling in the streets. Love and romance blossoming all over the place. Maybe there was something in the air, or in the water. The problem was she was breathing that air and drinking that water.

She'd looked at the girl Valentina had pointed out. "That's *very* short."

"I know, I like it. Do you think it will look nice on me?"

No doubt it would. With her pretty features, Valentina would look nice if she shaved her head bald and painted it purple.

Now Charli looked sideways at Valentina, seeing the thick dark hair shining like silk in the sunlight. It would be quite a step to cut that beautiful hair off. Of course she'd done the very thing herself not long ago and she wasn't sorry.

She gripped the keys in the pocket of her capris. They were almost at the apartment and she sent up a silent prayer to the god of good fortune, whoever that was, to please have the place not be a total ruin. Maybe she could even move in right away this afternoon. Get a taxi to take her and her suitcases over. She *so* wanted to *not* be in the same house with Massimo any longer.

Yesterday, Sunday, he'd been the perfect host. In the morning he had taken her and Valentina sailing and in the afternoon they'd gone for a drive so she could see something of the area. They'd driven through ancient seaside villages, visited the site of a Greek colony dating back to six hundred BC, and had a wonderful seafood dinner in an outdoor restaurant near the water. Valentina had been bored silly, but Charli had enjoyed sailing and exploring the countryside, and had been grateful for Valentina's presence.

She took the keys out of her pocket as they walked through the archway into the courtyard. The green door with its peeling paint beckoned her and she almost tripped on a loose stone as she rushed toward it.

The key turned easily enough and Valentina gave the door an enthusiastic shove. It opened into a stairwell, the stairs made of dull gray marble steps worn down by centuries of climbing feet. Even the air smelled old, and the light coming in through a dusty window looked gray and tired.

They rushed up several flights, past the door into another apartment and found the door marked with an old brass 2 in need of polishing. Apparently the ground floor did not count as number one.

"This is it," Valentina said unnecessarily.

The stairs climbed up one more flight, and the sounds of a television floated down to them. Charli found it a comforting thought that other people lived in this building. Taking a deep breath, she stuck the key in the lock and opened the door.

She stared, uncomprehending.

She'd had no idea what she'd find behind that door and she'd tried to be realistic. But of all the possibilities she'd imagined, this wasn't one of them.

CHAPTER FIVE

"You should have gone with them," Mimma said disapprovingly as she handed Massimo another tiny cup of *caffè*. "And you're drinking too much coffee in the morning. It's not good for your digestion."

The kitchen was fragrant with the scent of freshly baked *chitellini*—almond butter biscuits, or cookies, as Valentina would call them, imitating her American friend's American English. Massimo pulled up a chair and sat himself at the table and downed the offending beverage in a single swallow, then reached for one of the *chitellini*. He didn't feel like going back to his office. He was restless and couldn't concentrate on work. As a boy growing up in this house, he'd always gravitated toward the kitchen when he was in trouble with his parents, or just wanted a sympathetic ear. Mimma had always been there. She had listened to him, fed him fruit and pastries. It always smelled so wonderful in the kitchen.

"Why didn't you go with them?" she demanded when he did not answer her.

He shrugged. "It was not necessary, in my opinion. Charli is perfectly capable of collecting a key and taking possession of an apartment. And Valentina is with her in case there is a need for translation." Besides, Charli hadn't asked him.

He felt a ripple of irritation. When the phone call had come this morning she'd practically burst with enthusiasm.

"Maybe I can even move in today!" she'd said, her

sapphire eyes big as the sky. And she'd rushed right out, as if eager to escape. He gritted his teeth. She *was* eager to escape. What was it about that woman that drove him crazy? And why did she make such an effort to stay out of his way? What was she afraid of?

He watched Mimma clean a baby octopus, working quickly and efficiently from many years of practice. Tonight there'd be *insalata di polpo* on the menu, octopus salad. He wondered if Charli would be there to eat it. Surely that apartment wasn't near ready to be occupied after having been empty for a year.

"Do you think Charli will like octopus?" His experience with the eating habits of American women did not give him much hope. Even the sight of a perfectly nice whole fish, head still attached, made them squeamish.

Mimma gave him a deprecating look. "In case you haven't noticed, she likes everything I cook."

Right she was. He smiled at her. "Of course. What was I thinking?"

"She's a lovely young woman. She asked me to teach her how to cook Italian dishes, and she likes to help me in the kitchen."

No better way to get into Mimma's heart than that, for sure.

Mimma took another small octopus from the bowl. "Giulia, she was never in my kitchen."

"Cooking was not one of Giulia's talents," he said evenly. He didn't want to think about Giulia and her talents. He did not want to feel what he felt when he thought of her at all. It was in the past and it was much better for his peace of mind if it stayed there.

Mimma did not look up from her work. "You like Charli."

"I do?"

She looked up to meet his gaze. "I am old. I am not blind."

"You're not old. You're only sixty-two."

"You're changing the subject. I think you should find a wife. A man like you, it's no good to be without a wife." She frowned at him. "Why don't you find a wife? Giulia, she's been dead now a long time."

"You keep asking me that, Mimma. I don't want to get married again."

Mimma made an impatient gesture, waving her hand around, the knife slashing through the air. "What nonsense! There are plenty of good women to marry."

He said nothing, knowing what was coming.

"You think there are no good women left? You think all women are bad?" She launched into a fervent monologue about good women and bad women, and about good men and bad men, and how he was a *good* man and he deserved a *good* wife. Surely he wanted *bambini*, didn't he? And here he was, already far into his thirties, and surely it was time for him to get wise. And the women in Roma that he associated with, perhaps they were too loose and no good—

And so on and so forth.

He'd heard this speech numerous times and he let it flow over him like water, not really even hearing it anymore.

A good wife.

Surely if one wanted a wife, a good one would be the kind to have. But what was good? Mimma's requirements were simple: a good wife would like to cook and bear him children. But these were modern times and cooking talents were not a requirement. And the bearing of children was an issue to discuss. He did not need children to work his vineyard or plow his fields. So, theoretically speaking, what would he want?

A woman he could trust. A woman with loyalty and integrity. A woman who loved him enough to not die and— He stopped himself. Forget it. The issue was closed.

He pushed his chair back from the table. Mimma gave him a despairing look. "I say the rosary! I ask the Blessed Mother for her help! I light candles for you! Soon I will pray to San Giuda and Santa Rita!"

Patron saints of hopeless and desperate causes. He smiled and kissed her on the cheek. "If it makes you feel better, go ahead."

He glanced at his watch and wondered when Valentina and Charli would come back. If they'd found the apartment liveable.

No matter what, Charli would leave sooner or later, but she'd still be right here in town.

He didn't want a wife, but that didn't mean he didn't want Charli.

What he needed to do was find out why she kept resisting him.

Something was wrong. Charli stood at the door of the apartment and stared at the white Nikes on the floor underneath the coat rack. Further along she looked straight into the sitting room full of heavy, old-fashioned furniture. Sunlight slanted into one of the windows, setting on fire a bouquet of bright red flowers on the coffee table. The light slipped over a stack of books, a coffee cup and a laptop computer.

"Are you sure this is the right apartment?" Valentina asked, her voice incredulous.

"Apartment number two. I have the keys, and they

worked. The doors open. Yes, it is the right apartment. It's the right address!''

They both still stood in the doorway, uncertain as to whether they should enter.

''Well, somebody's living here,'' Valentina said, stating the obvious.

Charli was stunned. She had no idea what to think now. She took a hesitant step into the entryway. Nobody was home, that was clear. She clenched the keys in her hand. ''I don't believe this,'' she said. ''I mean, how can this be?''

''Maybe this great-aunt of yours didn't actually die.''

Charli gave her a look. ''Right, and maybe at the age of 95 she plays solitaire on the computer.'' She pointed at the sneakers. ''And she goes to the gym every day for a workout.''

Valentina laughed. ''I was joking, you know.''

''I hope so.'' Charli took a deep breath. ''Okay, I'm going to have a quick look around. It *is* my place and I *do* have the keys, so I'm *not* trespassing.'' She knew she was trying to convince herself of that. The person living here was a trespasser, a squatter, even if it was a person who liked fresh flowers.

''Look at this,'' Valentina said, frowning down at a map that lay spread out on the sofa. ''Uzbekistan! A girl in my school is from there.''

It felt odd, looking through the apartment of a stranger, someone she had never known. It was all neat and tidy but full of knick-knacks that looked a hundred years old. Maybe they were a hundred years old. In the kitchen there was a bowl of fruit on the counter—peaches, plums and grapes, dishes in the drain rack, half a loaf of bread in a plastic bag, a glass bowl with two balls of fresh mozzarella floating in water.

Never put fresh mozzarella in the fridge, Valentina had told her, translating Mimma's instructions. There was a balcony off the kitchen and through the glass door she glimpsed clay pots with cactus plants. They looked quite primordial with their contorted shapes and evil-looking spikes.

There were two bedrooms, and one of them was in use. A cobalt-blue suitcase stood in the corner. An expensive-looking digital camera lay on the dressing table and a pair of white linen slacks lay draped over a chair, with a pair of strappy white sandals underneath.

The squatter was a woman.

In the old-fashioned bathroom, toiletries stood lined up on a narrow ledge and a sexy purple bra hung over one of the towel racks. Probably not her great-aunt's either.

"We'd better get out of here," Valentina whispered, clearly not feeling comfortable about their inspection tour of the apartment.

A few minutes later they were outside again. Charli blinked against the bright sunlight and fished her new sunglasses out of her pocket. She stared up at the balcony she now knew to be hers. Helpless anger gripped her and she cursed under her breath.

"I'm going back to the *notaio's* office right now," she said. "They'd better figure out what is wrong here."

Valentina shook her head. "It will be closed. I heard that assistant woman say she's only there until twelve."

Charli felt an overwhelming sense of defeat. Only ten minutes ago she'd climbed those stairs feeling as if she was on a high, and now her spirits had crashed. How could this all be so complicated? Why was nothing working the way it was supposed to? What did she have to do to get into her own apartment? To get away from Massimo?

"Come on, let's go home," Valentina said. "Massimo will know what to do."

The words were meant to comfort her, Charli knew, but in reality they only made her angrier. She didn't *want* to ask Massimo what to do. She wanted to take care of her own business, deal with her own problems.

It was just past noon and the Mediterranean sun blasted down without mercy. She was hot and thirsty and angry. A headache threatened behind her eyes.

With a defeated sigh she followed Valentina down the narrow street, back up through the alleys full of washing, up the stone steps that climbed the hill, back to the cool villa.

A shower revived her and she was drying her hair with a towel when a knock came on her door.

"Come in," she called out and Massimo entered.

"Oh, I thought you were Valentina." She tossed the towel on the bed.

"Lunch will be ready in twenty minutes," he said.

She nodded. "Thank you."

He studied her and she felt ridiculously self-conscious standing there in her bare feet with nothing but a skimpy little bathrobe on.

"Valentina told me what happened," he said.

She tightened the belt. "I'll call the office again later. Maybe they know what happened."

"I doubt it. Nobody is supposed to be in there. You're the owner."

Impatiently, she wiped at a drop of water sliding down her cheek. "Then I'll go back to the apartment later this afternoon and wait to see who's there and talk to them— her. It's a woman."

He pushed his hands in his trouser pockets. "I'll sort it out for you. I'll make some calls."

He was just trying to be helpful, and she tried not to be annoyed. "No," she said tightly. "I mean, I should be able to take care of this myself." She swallowed. "Thank you, though, for offering."

"It's not a big deal, Charli."

"Well, it is for me! None of this is working out the way I had planned."

"Is this causing you a real problem? What had you planned?"

She threw her hands in the air, caught herself making the gesture. "I had expected to be in the place by now! To not be…"

"Is it so terrible to stay here? To be my guest?" He moved a little closer.

"It's not that. I appreciate your hospitality, truly. It's…I don't like feeling that I'm not in charge of things, to be so *dependent*. That there's no place to go."

He laughed and she glared at him.

"It's not funny!"

"Are you not a little melodramatic? I'm not holding you captive, am I?"

"Well, no, of course not." He was standing right in front of her. She wiped away another vagrant drop of water and looked down at her bare toes.

She felt his hands on her arms. "Relax, Charli."

Her heart began an uneasy rhythm and before she could react he had slipped his arms around her and her head ended up on his shoulder. She didn't resist, and she knew she should, really, but she was tired and discouraged and it felt nice to be held. It was a very good feeling. Much too good for the moment and the occasion.

"It wouldn't be a bad fantasy, come to think of it," he

whispered in her ear. "I'd lock the door, keep the key, and every night I'd come to you and make passionate…"

She pulled back, out of his embrace, and glared at him. "Over my dead body!"

He grinned. "I'm joking, Charli. At least about the key."

"I should hope so." She crossed her arms in front of her chest. "And you'd better be joking about the passionate whatever, too."

He studied her. "So, who kept you imprisoned, if I may ask? That former lover of yours?"

"No! What kind of question is that?"

He shrugged. "You seem to be overly sensitive about the issue."

"Overly sensitive?" She took another step away from him. "Because I don't want to be…to be dependent on your goodwill? Because I don't like feeling that I can't figure things out for myself?" Her body was tense with nerves.

"Why is it so terrible to accept help from me?"

She took a steadying breath. "It's against my personal rules." She flopped down on the side of the bed.

"Your personal rules? Rules for what?"

"Rules for living my own life," she said, her voice tight. "For being independent."

His shrug was pure Italian—easy, casual. "Everybody needs help sometimes. It's perfectly normal. It doesn't mean you're incapable or incompetent, Charli."

"Thank you."

"You're in a foreign country. You don't speak the language. Surely you're not—"

"And here you are, all ready to take charge of my problems. To help the maiden in distress." It gave her satisfaction to see the annoyance flashing across his face.

"You make it sound like a crime. I am a man, Charli. I see a maiden in distress, and out come my natural gentlemanly instincts, my normal Italian helpfulness, and—"

"...your natural desire to seduce me."

"That wasn't what I was going to say, but yes, the thought has occurred to me that...ah...a bit of seduction might be a pleasant mutual experience." He moved closer to the bed. She didn't like it.

"I told you before, I'm not interested."

He stood in front of her and stared down into her eyes. "Are you afraid I'll demand sexual favors as reciprocation for helping you?"

"You're a man, aren't you?"

He held her challenging gaze for a long moment. "Not that kind of a man."

She felt a moment of embarrassment. Good grief, what was she thinking? "I suppose you don't need to...do a lot of bargaining and haggling to get women in your bed."

"Bargaining and haggling?" He arched one eyebrow. "You mean like over the price of...peaches, cherries?"

"Or meat." She bit her lip, controlling the sudden urge to smile.

He gave a careless shrug. "To answer your question, no. I do not bargain or haggle. I prefer women who come to me willingly." He moved closer, standing right in front of her. "However, a bit of seduction beforehand can be amusing." He stroked her cheek in a slow feathering caress and her pulse leaped. "Don't you agree?"

She'd made a mistake sitting down on the bed, she realized. There was no way to escape with him standing right in front of her. He put his hands on her shoulders and nudged her enough so she lost her balance and fell backward. He leaned over, placed his hands on the bed beside her face and balanced his body over hers, not touching.

"I'll scream," she said, her voice low with threat.

"Yes, I have that effect on women when they're in the throes of passion," he said deadpan.

"I am *not* in the throes—" She stopped herself, saw the glint of humor in his eyes. She bit her lip and turned her face away. "Get off of me," she said tightly.

"I'm not even touching you."

"What do you want me to do? Beg you?"

"No, that would be so undignified." He offered her his most charming smile. "Kiss me. Prove to me you're not interested and not willing and I'll let you go. Gentleman's honor."

"I'm not interested and not willing. My word should be enough."

"You're lying, *cara*." He said it very softly, lowering his face a little. She closed her eyes, clenched her teeth and said nothing.

Gently, very gently, he touched his lips to hers, then teased her lips with the tip of his tongue, slipping into her mouth as her lips softened. She gave a little moan—of protest or pleasure or both, and a dizzying desire rushed wildly through her.

He reached his arm under her shoulders and drew her further onto the bed and lowered himself on top of her. She gave no resistance, yielded to him, kissing him back, and she was aware that she could easily lose all control.

He rolled away from her suddenly. Sat up and looked at her face, then lowered his gaze. She glanced down, saw her robe gaping open at the top, exposing one bare breast, the nipple hard and raspberry pink. She reached up to cover herself, feeling…she didn't know what she was feeling. Her body ached and trembled and she hated him for doing this to her so easily.

He got off the bed, raked his hand through his hair and marched to the door, leaving without a word.

"Where's Charli?" Valentina asked impatiently. "I'm starving."

Massimo took a slice of mozzarella and shrugged. "She'll be here in a minute."

After leaving her room he'd taken a cold shower, cursing himself for being an idiot. It had helped cool his blood, but he was beginning to wonder what reaction Charli was having to their little tussle on the bed. Surely by now she'd recuperated and put her clothes on.

Where was she?

Valentina bounced out of her chair. "I'll go get her."

He leaned back in his chair and his cellphone rang. He fished it out of his pocket and flipped it open. "*Pronto*."

"Massimo! It's Elena. *Come sta*?"

Oh, God, not Elena. He closed his eyes and searched for patience. "I'm fine, thanks."

"You sound tired. Poor you. Is Valentina giving you problems? Teenagers these days, they are so much trouble. I can only imagine what it must be like for you. I was thinking you should—"

"She's gone!" Valentina came bursting into the dining room and he didn't hear what other wisdoms Elena was offering up for his benefit.

"Elena," he said into the phone, interrupting her, "thank you for your insights. I'll call you back later." He cut the connection without waiting for her reply.

Valentina flung her hands up in a gesture of frustration. "I looked everywhere! Mimma hasn't seen her, either. What did you do? What did you say to her?"

An honest reply to this would not benefit his seventeen-year-old sister. "Calm down, Valentina. She probably decided to go back to town to see about the apartment."

"We just came from there! And you told me you'd help her!" It sounded like an accusation and he felt a stirring of anger. Of frustration.

"She didn't want my help," he said flatly. "Sit down and let's eat."

Valentina plopped down on her chair and tossed her hair back over her shoulder and gave him a challenging look. "Why would she leave without eating first? I don't get it."

"Maybe she wasn't hungry. I'm not a mind-reader, Valentina." He held out the salad plate to her. "Here, have some of this."

She glowered at him, clearly suspicious, but she dropped the subject. Instead she started talking about a grammar school friend who'd just come back to town from a holiday trip. They wanted to go to the outdoor concert tonight, have something to eat in town, was that all right? Fine, he said. Gina was a nice girl. He'd known her family here in town since he was a boy.

He ate without tasting anything. He kept thinking about Charli, seeing her as she'd lain there on the bed, all soft and willing, one perky breast inviting him with its rosy nipple. He looked down at his dessert and almost groaned. Sweet, ripe, luscious raspberries.

Charli was sitting on the top step of the stairs near the front door of the apartment, elbows braced on her knees, her head in her hands, waiting. Stewing. Sooner or later that woman would have to come home and she was not leaving until she did. She was going to sit here all night if necessary. At least the old marble was cool to sit on if the rest of the stairwell was muggy and warm.

The smell of cooking drifted down from upstairs. Onions, garlic, oregano. It smelled wonderful and her stomach growled. She was starving. After Massimo had left her room she couldn't bear to face him again over lunch, so she'd skipped out of the house and gone down to town and wandered around in a trance of fury and embarrassment. She was a weakling.

She groaned and shifted on the cold marble, pushing the memories of her total cave-in away.

The door downstairs squeaked open and she lifted her head. Maybe the trespassing witch was coming home. She was ready for battle. But it wasn't a woman coming up the stairs. It was a man. Massimo.

"I thought I might find you here," he said, his voice cool as spring water.

Every muscle in her body tensed. "What do you want?"

"I want to apologize."

She put her hand on her chest. "Be still my heart."

"I didn't intend to upset you."

"Oh, please, spare me." She looked away from him.

"I was worried about you when you didn't come to lunch," she heard him say. "I looked all over for you."

She couldn't believe what she was hearing. "Worried, why? You thought I'd thrown myself off the cliffs or something?"

"You do have a sense of the dramatic, don't you?"

"Italy brings it out in me." For effect she flung her hands in the air. "Must be the air, the water."

"Where have you been all afternoon?"

She shrugged. "Everywhere."

She'd walked all over town, found the *studio di notaio*

closed. Of course it had been. Most businesses and shops were closed in the afternoon and wouldn't open again until five. She'd checked at the tourist office at the railroad station and had been told there still were no rooms available in town. She'd gone to the apartment and found no one there. She'd waited for an hour and then walked down to the marina and watched the boats and ferries come and go. Now she was back at the apartment, waiting again, and this time she wasn't leaving.

Massimo lowered himself on the step below, turning sideways to look at her. She didn't want him here. She waved her hand. "Please, make yourself at home," she said sarcastically.

"Thank you," he said soberly.

She glared at him. "I didn't actually mean that."

"I didn't think so."

She groaned and closed her eyes. "Please, go away."

"Charli, I'm sorry. I didn't mean to—"

"You didn't mean what? Oh, please, you exactly meant what you did! So I hope you're happy. You proved your point. You're a master of seduction and I'm easy. Now leave me alone so I can suffer my humiliation in peace."

Her stomach growled audibly, which did nothing for her sense of dignity.

He arched one eyebrow. "Humiliation?"

She gritted her teeth. "Don't tell me I am overreacting."

"There's no reason for you to feel humiliated."

"Well, I'm not used to feeling like…like I'm full of cheap lust and ripe for the plucking by any man who—" Oh, God, she heard herself say the words, saw him struggle not to laugh.

She dropped her head in her hands, wishing she could

just die right there. Could she embarrass herself any more?

He said nothing, made not a sound.

From the apartment above came the noise of playing children, music—the familiar tune of *Old MacDonald had a farm*. She heard it on the fringes of her consciousness, wondered vaguely what Italian children would make of the English song. Well, it wouldn't be in English, of course. It would have been translated.

He was touching her, taking away her hands.

"Charli, come home with me. You cannot stay here."

She pulled her hands out of his grasp. "Yes I can. I'm going to sit here until she comes back—that woman, whoever she is."

"Her name is Antonia Graziani. And she's not coming back here tonight."

CHAPTER SIX

AT UNEXPECTED moments Charli's mind would flash back to her relationship with Richard. One of his control freak tactics had been not telling her things. Seemingly innocent little things that would throw off her own plans or cause other inconveniences. He'd always be so sorry, of course, and it had never really been his fault somehow and then he'd try to make her feel guilty for being upset. Making her feel guilty was another little skill he had.

Memories of his various manipulations rushed into Charli's head as she sat in front of her apartment door, stunned by Massimo's announcement.

Her name is Antonia Graziani. And she's not coming back here tonight.

She stared at him as his words hung suspended in the air between them and wild imaginings sprouted in her head like weeds. She remembered the lacy purple bra in the bathroom, the sexy white sandals.

"You *know* her?" she finally managed to ask. "You know all about this and you didn't tell me?" She clambered to her feet, her legs wobbly with rage and light-headedness. She put her hand against the grungy wall for support. It would not do to crash down the stairs and break a few bones. Talk about being helpless.

He stood as well and frowned down at her. "Don't overreact, Charli. I—"

"What kind of game are you playing with me, Massimo? Who is this woman?"

Annoyance flickered in his eyes. "I'm not playing any

games,'' he said flatly. ''I'll tell you what I know, but not here in this Godforsaken stairwell.'' He grabbed her hand. ''Let's get out of here.''

His grip on her was pure steel and, unless she intended to crumple and break something, she'd better keep her balance and follow the commander down the stairs.

He practically dragged her outside, through the archway, into the street.

''Let go of me!'' She yanked at his hand, but he did not let go.

Which was a good thing. A sudden wave of dizziness washed over her and she teetered for a moment, holding on to him for dear life.

''*Dio!*'' He released her hand and put his arm around her, holding her steady. ''What is wrong? Are you ill?''

''No, no. It's nothing very dramatic.'' She sucked in a deep breath. ''Just low blood sugar. I didn't have lunch.''

''I take full responsibility for that,'' he said gravely, as if owning up to a crime of major proportions.

''You're a gentleman.''

He frowned at her, as if not sure if she was serious or not. Then he began walking again, his arm still around her shoulders. ''There's a place over there,'' he said, motioning toward the outdoor *caffè* visible at the corner of the street.

It was not easy admitting to herself that she liked the secure feel of his arm around her, but she decided not to dwell on it, simply accept it as a convenience in case her brain had ambitions to go spinning again.

Fortunately she reached the coffee shop in conscious mode and minutes after she sat down she was presented with a cup of cappuccino and a plate of five different pastries—enough sugar to last her through the rest of the month.

She bit into a crunchy *sfogliatella*, a regional specialty, and one of her favorite pastries. It was filled with a sweet ricotta cream and she felt the sweetness slide down her throat, into her famished stomach. Ah, bliss.

She sighed and sat back, took a drink from the cappuccino.

"Are you all right?" he asked, still the perfect gentleman.

"Yes, of course." Physically speaking, at least.

"Have another one," he suggested, pushing the plate closer to her.

"Oh, I will." She reached for a *cornetti* filled with chocolate. Very yummy too. For a few moments she simply concentrated on eating. She finished her cappuccino, wiped her mouth and glanced over at Massimo.

He wore one of those Italian shirts with bold stripes, no tie, sleeves rolled up. His hair lay swept back in lazy waves, teasing the top of his shirt collar at the back of his neck. He looked impossibly, sexily Italian. He was drinking a beer, looking calm and relaxed.

She sighed, no longer hungry. The sugar was skiing right into her bloodstream, from where it danced straight into her brain. She felt her energy returning, and with it her annoyance at his high-handedness.

"So, who's that woman in my apartment? Why do you know her? Are you involved in some conspiracy to keep me from moving into my apartment?"

He raised his brows in silent reproof.

She shot him a killer look. "Don't say it."

"Say what?"

That I'm a drama queen. "Never mind. Just tell me about Antonia what's-her-name. How do you know her?"

"I don't know her. I never even met her." He took

another swallow of beer. "All I did was ask one of the neighbor ladies about her."

"I don't get it. When was that?"

"This afternoon, after lunch. I went looking for you and I first went to the apartment but you weren't there. I talked to the woman upstairs. She was very helpful."

Charli felt stupid. Why hadn't she talked to the woman upstairs? Possibly she spoke enough English. Why had it not even occurred to her to do that?

"And what did she say?" She wiped her sugary fingers on a paper napkin.

"She says this Antonia is some family member who used to visit your great-aunt once in a while. She—the neighbor lady—spoke to her yesterday and Antonia said she was going to Naples for business and would be back tomorrow afternoon."

A family member. That accounted for the fact that she had keys. This did not look good.

Charli clenched her hands in her lap. "She must think she owns the apartment."

"One doesn't just own an apartment, Charli."

Well, no, of course not, and she had the paperwork to prove it. "But that woman must be thinking she has some right to be there!"

He nodded. "So it appears."

Charli sighed with frustration. "Well, I'll have to find a way to get her out of there. I suppose I can simply go in, throw her stuff out the door, change the locks and move in myself."

"Yes, you could do that." The tone of his voice indicated he did not judge this to be a sound course of action.

Charli considered the laptop, the digital camera, the purple bra, the red flowers, the cobalt blue suitcase and the yellow map of Uzbekistan. She visualized them sitting in a rainbow-colored heap outside the green painted door in the courtyard. Not a way to make friends, probably. Then again, this wasn't about making friends, was it?

Two soft brown pigeons scampered around her feet, looking for crumbs. The Duomo bells chimed six o'clock, then continued playing a joyous tune, a lovely old-world sound.

Here she was, in this charming Italian town, and she didn't feel very joyous at all. A squatter was living in her apartment and—

Squatter. The word struck terror in her heart. The apartment had been empty for a year now—or so she'd assumed. "What about squatter's rights?" she asked. "You must have a law here in Italy."

One corner of his mouth kicked up in amusement. "Of course, but isn't it a tad premature to worry about that at this time?" He sounded so calm, so reasonable, so...*un*-Italian. Where was his hot-blooded Italian passion when she wanted it?

Not a good train of thought. The memory of his passion only hours ago flashed through her mind. She looked away from him, reached blindly for another pastry and took a bite.

"Would you like another coffee? Something else?"

She shook her head and put the pastry down. She was going to make herself sick with all this rich sugary stuff.

A young couple with a small boy strolled by, the woman all dressed up in high heels and a long white skirt, all three licking ice-cream cones and looking relaxed.

Massimo put his glass down. "Shall we go then?"

They drove back to the villa in Massimo's car, hair blowing in the wind. The road snaking up and around the rocky hills offered glorious vistas of the Mediterranean. The sun hung low in the sky, washing the landscape in golden light. Oleander and bougainvillea bloomed in jewel colors amid the verdant green of palms and trees. The air smelled of sea and sun, of lemons and flowers, of love and seduction.

It was like a movie, she thought. Charli glanced sideways at Massimo, his profile silhouetted against the sky— forehead, nose and chin carved in strong lines like a marble statue of some powerful Roman emperor. It seemed unreal that she was sitting next to this paragon of masculine sex-appeal, zipping along a most gloriously beautiful stretch of Italian coast.

He was movie-star handsome, he wanted her, and she was going home with him.

What was wrong with this picture?

"What are you going to do if that woman says she's not leaving?" Valentina asked Charli as they made their way back to the apartment the next afternoon. A Vespa zoomed past them in the narrow alley.

Charli had asked herself that question ever since she'd gone back to the villa with Massimo the night before. She had no idea what she'd do, what her options were if she of the purple bra and the map of Uzbekistan refused to vacate the premises. Go to the police?

"I don't know, Valentina." Charli wiped her hand over her damp forehead. It was four-thirty in the afternoon and still hotter than blazes.

"Why won't you let Massimo handle it? He's good at that stuff, you know."

"I don't doubt it, but he's a busy man and I should take care of my own problems." This sounded very good, very responsible, but Charli had secret doubts about her ability to negotiate the infamously convoluted workings of the Italian bureaucracy. Massimo's help might well be necessary if she couldn't get the woman to leave peacefully.

Last night Valentina had gone to a concert with a friend and she'd been alone with Massimo at dinner. All evening he'd been the model of courtesy, a veritable master of decorum. Not a dubious word had passed his lips as they drove home, no unseemly look had come her way as dinner progressed through its various courses. Instead of calming the vibrations between them, it had only made the tension worse. The wine hadn't helped either and by the time *dolce* had arrived, in the form of chilled coffee cream, she had been a nervous wreck.

Claiming a headache, she'd excused herself and taken refuge in her room. Never before had a man so unsettled her. It was pathetic. It was ridiculous.

Never before have you wanted a man as much as you want Massimo, came the unbidden thought. *Admit it, girl.*

Charli gritted her teeth in frustration, turned the corner into a narrow alley and almost tripped over an uneven cobblestone.

"Slow down," Valentina said. "You're racing like you're running laps."

Charli stood still to catch her breath. "Sorry, I was just thinking." Ahead the alley climbed up to the Duomo, the view of the church partially obscured by jeans and shirts drying on a washing line strung high across the alley.

Valentina gave a little laugh. "It's all that adrenaline because you're angry with that woman for stealing your apartment."

"Probably." Charli pushed her sunglasses up and started moving again. They were almost there. She hoped the squatter spoke enough English to appreciate the full meaning of the speech she had prepared in her mind. It would be so lame to do it all in translation.

In the courtyard, she glanced up at the balcony and caught a flash of reflected sunlight in the glass of the closing door. Somebody was there.

She didn't bother to ring the downstairs bell, but opened the green door with her key and moved up the stairs to apartment number two, Valentina right behind her.

Her heart was beating fast as she knocked on the door.

CHAPTER SEVEN

NOT a moment after Charli knocked, the door was flung open and she found herself face to face with a tall woman clutching a silver cellphone to her ear. She was barefoot, wearing loose white linen slacks and a sleeveless purple shirt. With her short black hair, huge violet eyes, Antonia Graziani was stunning.

"Entri! Entri!" She moved aside, smiled widely, waved her free hand in invitation and continued talking in rapid Italian into the phone.

For a moment Charli was too shocked to move, then she stepped inside, followed by Valentina.

As she continued her conversation, Antonia Graziani kept on smiling at them as if they were treasured guests. She gestured into the sitting room, motioned them to sit down and turned her back to close the front door.

Valentina leaned her head close to Charli's. "I *love* her hair!" she whispered. Charli almost laughed out loud. Leave it to a teenager to think about *hair* at a time like this.

"Ciao, grazie," Antonia said into the phone and flipped it shut as she graced the two of them with another wide, welcoming smile. "I'm so happy to see you!" she said, as if she had long expected to find them at the door. "You must be Charli Olson, yes?" She held out her hand. "I'm Antonia Graziani."

They shook hands and then Valentina introduced herself.

"Si accomodi! Sit down, please!" Antonia indicated a

red overnight bag. "I just arrived ten minutes ago and found the note under the door. Let me fetch some drinks from the kitchen. I shall only be a moment." She swept out of the room, leaving Charli and Valentina looking at each other in stunned silence.

One thing at least was perfectly clear: Antonia spoke English.

"What note?" Valentina whispered. "And how does she know who you are?"

"Massimo told me he left it yesterday." Charli glanced around the room. It was just the way she had seen it yesterday except for the red overnight bag.

Antonia came back carrying a tray with stemless wineglasses and three tiny green bottles. "You like *frizzante*, yes? Or do you prefer water?" They said *frizzante* was just fine. Antonia placed the tray on the coffee table, sat down, and proceeded to unscrew the caps and pour the fizzy white wine into the glasses, her movements smooth and elegant.

Each bottle held a mere small glass of wine, came in a six-pack, and had a screw cap. And that in Italy, a place where wine and food were held sacred. When Charli had first seen the bottles she'd been tempted to write to Richard, he of the wine snobbery. *Guess what they have in Italy! Wine in six-packs! Bottles with screw caps!*

The wine was cool and delicious in spite of its déclassé packaging, at least to her unsophisticated palate.

"I was *so* worried!" Antonia said. "I didn't know where you were. I checked the hotels and you weren't anywhere. I thought perhaps you had gone back to America and—"

A dizzying waterfall of words flowed over them. Something about her uncle in the hospital, a plane to Moscow, a husband waiting. Charli couldn't get a word in crosswise and gave up. She drank her wine and tried to piece together a story that became more convoluted by the minute.

Apparently Antonia did not live in Italy, but moved around from place to place with a diplomat husband who was presently in Moscow for reasons unexplained. Her parents lived in Florida, also for reasons unexplained. Antonia was related to the *notaio*, who'd been somehow related to the husband of Charli's great-aunt who had been a sweet lady with whom Antonia had stayed sometimes when she had been in the country for a spell of things Italian. Her parents-in-law were terrible people, *orribili*, and she didn't want to stay with them because it was bad for her nerves and she came to Italy to relax.

Or something like that.

Charli's head was spinning, but not from low blood sugar. Even Valentina looked dazed.

Antonia sighed deeply. The last few months had been *so* exhausting, she went on, gesticulating with her elegant hand, and she'd come to the apartment because, well, she was homeless, really, and she was so tired after much travelling and doing boring things with her diplomat husband and she wanted to be alone for a while to relax and to find some old photographs if they were still somewhere among this clutter and she'd thought the place was empty and she hadn't known it now belonged to her, Charli, until yesterday. And really, she was *so* sorry if she'd done something wrong. She stopped to catch her breath. Even Charli found herself without air just from listening to her.

Antonia rushed out to the kitchen to get more wine, came back with a big bottle rather than more small ones and opened it with great expertise while her mouth went on and on and on…

"When I picked up the keys yesterday," Charli said,

squeezing in her words while Antonia took a second to breathe, "the woman didn't say anything about you being here."

Antonia rolled her eyes and threw her hands up in an expression of utter disgust. "She was that new woman, yes? The one who is helping out now with my uncle in hospital, and she knows nothing! She hadn't even asked you where you were staying, where to find you! I could not telephone you! I was so...*arrabiata*! Furious! I waited. I called the hotels and could not find you and I had to go to Napoli..."

They barely made it back to the villa in time for dinner. Valentina, eyes sparkling with excitement, couldn't wait to bring Massimo up to date and launched into an animated account of the visit.

"Massimo, she is gorgeous! Like a model! You should have seen her hair! And she lives in Uzbekistan! She's going back on Friday, but she's first going to Moscow and..."

Massimo let her talk, calmly eating his *parmigiana di melanzane*—a lyrical-sounding name for what Charli knew as eggplant parmesan.

Charli watched Massimo, knowing this would be the last meal they would eat together at the villa. Tomorrow morning she would get her bags ready, call a taxi and move into the apartment. She'd told Antonia it was no problem for her to stay until Friday. She'd help her look for the photographs, and Antonia had said she'd initiate her into the mysterious workings of the water heater.

In the candlelight Massimo's face looked dark and brooding. Or maybe it was just her imagination. He looked up from his plate.

''So no need to hire a lawyer and start eviction procedures?''

Charli didn't miss the faint mockery in his voice, but pretended not to notice it.

Valentina's eyes grew large. ''Oh, no, she's not stealing the apartment at all. Actually, you know…''

Charli let Valentina do most of the talking. It was easier that way and Valentina was having fun. Charli didn't feel much like talking. She was enjoying the food and the wine and trying desperately not to look at Massimo.

It was a lost cause, really. Her gaze wandered off in his direction without her consent, which probably had something to do with the wine she was drinking. And the fact that she'd had a couple of glasses already with Antonia. But this particular wine was very delicious, and it went down so nicely with the delicious food. Massimo looked so good. She loved looking at his chin, and his hands, and the strong column of his neck. He wore a white linen shirt, the collar unbuttoned, and she suddenly felt a bit sad, knowing that from now on she would be having her evening meals without the view of all that male splendor.

She wanted to touch him, and then she remembered what had happened when she had touched him last time. The feeling came rushing back and she had another drink of the wine and she felt so good and then Massimo looked at her and refilled her glass like the gentleman he was.

Later she lay in bed, realizing her capacity for wine had been surpassed. She wondered why Massimo hadn't taken the chance to further demonstrate his talent for seduction. She fell asleep before her fuzzy mind could formulate an answer.

*   *   *

When dawn came, Massimo had been up for hours. It had rained in the night, and when he looked out of his office window he saw more clouds hanging heavy in the gray sky.

Charli was packing up her things, Mimma informed him when he strolled into the kitchen for one more *caffè*. What a shame she was leaving, said Mimma. She expelled a long-suffering sigh and gave him an accusing look. She so enjoyed Charli's company and really she was quite good in the kitchen, which was surprising, wasn't it? From what she'd heard women in America didn't cook anymore. All they did was buy these awful ready-made meals in tins and jars and boxes, and those frozen horrors that were now all over the Italian supermarkets as well. Had he seen those bags of frozen *gnocchi*? What was the world coming to if a woman couldn't even make her own *gnocchi* anymore? It was terrible, didn't he agree? Pretty soon Italian women were going to give up cooking altogether, but she hoped they'd wait until she was dead.

He escaped the kitchen and made his way to Charli's room. The door stood open and her back was turned to him as she folded clothes into a suitcase on the bed. She was wearing a short skirt of some flouncy material and below the hem her slim legs were tanned and bare. His gaze lingered on her narrow ankles and small feet, also bare. He liked the delicate shape of her feet and toes, the luscious berry-pink of her nail polish. He surprised himself. Feet had never been of special interest to him.

He tapped his fingers on the door-frame and she turned around.

"Hi," she said, clutching some silky underwear to her chest.

"Good morning. You're packing, I see."

"Yes." She turned and dropped the bras and panties in

her suitcase and looked back at him again. "I thought I might as well get going." She wiped a curl away from her forehead. "Is Valentina up yet?"

"I haven't seen her." He leaned back against the doorframe. "She'll miss having you around, you know. And so will Mimma. She told me so a few minutes ago, in the kitchen. She gave me the evil eye because somehow she thinks it's my fault you're leaving."

"I was only here because I couldn't get into my apartment. She knows that."

A damp breeze blew in through the open window. The rain in the night had washed the dusty world and the temperature had dropped significantly since yesterday.

"You're welcome to stay here if you want to wait until that woman leaves on Friday."

"Thank you, but I really want to get over there. Antonia is going to tell me about some of the problems with the place, and show me the foibles of the water heater. And she has suggestions about making some renovations. The kitchen and the bathroom are rather old-fashioned and…anyway, I like her, so I think it might be fun having her around for a day or so."

"All right, as you wish." He couldn't keep her here against her will. Although his earlier fantasy of keeping her locked up in this room still held some wicked appeal. "When you're ready to go, let me know. I'll drive you over."

"Thank you, but that's not necessary. I called for a taxi."

He stiffened with irritation. Why did she have to be so damned standoffish? What had he done to deserve this? Last night he'd been a paragon of good behavior. He had not touched her, not kissed her, while knowing full well that he'd have no trouble at all seducing her if he gave it even half a try. It had nearly killed him to be such a saint.

He pushed himself away from the doorjamb. "Good God, woman, what is the matter with you? Why didn't you just ask me?"

She shrugged. "I didn't want to disturb you. You're working. I'm perfectly capable of finding transport. I may not know much, but that I can do."

He moved closer toward her. "Charli, are you so threatened by a man who wants you in his bed that you have to run away like this?"

She stiffened. "I'm not running away. And we already had this discussion."

A sudden gust of wind rushed in and slammed the door shut.

"Why not just let it happen? What is more natural than two people wanting each other? I'm not going to hurt you."

"How do you know?" Her eyes were clouded with doubt.

Well, he didn't know. What had made him ask that question? What was wrong with him? This woman spelled trouble. She had issues, as the expression went in English. Usually he had no patience for women and their "issues". They were too much trouble to deal with. His life was complicated enough and if a woman he might initially be interested in showed signs of making it more so, he simply refused to become involved.

"Tell me what worries you." Some other part of him was in charge—not the rational part that wanted things easy and simple in his life.

She crossed her arms protectively across her chest and tightened her chin. "It's craziness, Massimo! I'll be back in the States in a couple of months. Why do you even care? Why don't you find someone who's going to hang around longer?"

Well, yes, why not? Only this wasn't about being logical and practical, was it?

"Is this about rationalizing? Well, I don't know why. All I know is that…" He hesitated. "When I see you all I want to do is kiss you and hold you and make love to you. The world is full of women and I don't want any of them. I want you."

As if in blessing, the rain poured down in a soft rushing whoosh.

She looked down, saying nothing. He noticed her hand trembling.

He lifted her chin. "Charli?" he whispered.

She didn't move, her gaze meeting his, her eyes huge and jewel-blue, her berry-red lips full and slightly parted. Had she any idea how erotic she looked at this moment?

Desire spread like wildfire through him. She smelled of something sweet and fruity. And then he was tasting her, kissing her soft mouth, sliding his hands around her, under her shirt to feel the warm skin of her back.

She gave a feeble moan of protest, then melted into him almost instantly. He felt the soft warmth of her breasts through the thin fabric of his shirt. The blood pounded through his veins. The feel, the scent, the taste of her intoxicated his senses. He was losing his brain power in a hurry and he didn't care.

She was all luscious womanly temptation. He wanted her clothes off. He wanted her naked against him. His body throbbed and ached with need.

On the fringes of his consciousness he registered the honking of a car.

Moments later knocking on the door jerked him back to sanity. Charli pushed herself away from him as Valentina's voice called out to say the taxi had arrived.

More pounding. "Charli! Are you in there?"

He watched as Charli took a deep, tremulous breath and moved to the door and opened it. "I'm almost ready, Valentina," she said. "Would you mind getting my book for me? I think I left it on the coffee table in the living room."

He had to give her credit for thinking fast. Valentina in the room with them right now would not be a good thing. He closed his eyes for a moment and tried to collect a semblance of control.

Without looking at him, Charli moved over to the bed and closed her two suitcases.

"I'll carry them down for you," he said.

"Thank you," she said politely, still not looking at him.

Ten minutes later she climbed into the taxi after a flurry of hugs, kisses and goodbyes to the three of them. He watched the car disappear around the first bend of the serpentine road, still feeling the polite peck she'd offered him with her thanks.

He rubbed his chest and let out a weary breath. It was better this way, he thought. In his relationships with women he wanted things simple. And with Charli...well, it wouldn't be simple.

His chest felt tight. It felt as if something inside him was trying to break loose, some live thing shackled and trapped and frightened. Impatient with himself, he turned on his heel and strode inside.

CHAPTER EIGHT

CHARLI was sitting on her balcony working on her laptop, sipping *frizzante*. She'd been in her apartment for almost a week now. Antonia had left and she was enjoying her solitude. She glanced over at the Duomo, waiting for the bells to start ringing out the hour of four. But it wasn't the Duomo bells that rang first, but her phone, and to her surprise it was Bree.

"Good news and bad news," Bree said. "My computer crashed."

"And that wouldn't be the good news."

Bree sighed heavily. "No."

The good news was that she'd found the perfect person to rent Charli's apartment. Her cousin Mindy from Minnesota. Apparently the poor girl was going through a nasty break-up with her man and was depressed. She was also in the process of writing her doctoral dissertation and desperately needed a haven away from her own environment to finish the project.

"You are still wanting to rent it out, right?" Bree asked.

"Yes, sure, after I leave in a couple of months and the kitchen and bathroom are fixed up."

"Good. I think Italy might be good for her," Bree said. "Maybe she can find herself a romantic Italian lover to cheer her up."

A blue Vespa came roaring into the courtyard, stopped. A man in a suit and tie jumped off, whipped the helmet

96

off his curly dark head and strode through one of the decrepit-looking doors.

''By the way, did you get the pictures before your computer crashed?'' Charli asked. She'd e-mailed Bree photos of the apartment taken with her digital camera.

''Yes, I did. Clearly a very cute place, but the kitchen needs work. But what I really wanted was a picture of your Latin lover. Men are so much more interesting than kitchens, or cacti, although I must say those cacti are impressive. Very primordial-looking.''

''He's not my Latin lover, and he would not take kindly to my taking a picture of him to show off to my friends.''

Bree groaned. ''I don't believe you,'' she said, ''saying no to this man.''

Charli sighed, trying not to think of Massimo kissing her. ''Sometimes I don't believe myself, either.''

The problem was, she was always thinking of Massimo kissing her. Half an hour later she was climbing the hill to the villa and thinking about Massimo kissing her. She was going to his house because she'd been stupid enough to leave some clothes in the dryer when she had packed her things last week and she needed them. She really hoped she wasn't going to run into him.

Please don't let me run into him, she pleaded to whatever deity was willing to grant her the request. It was silly, really. Surely she could face him for a few minutes without any emotional drama and trauma?

Mimma was all smiles when Charli walked into the kitchen. Then Valentina sashayed in and Charli gaped at her.

''Valentina! I hardly recognized you!''

Valentina laughed. ''Do you like it?'' She twirled around to give Charli a full view of her now very short hairdo. Very short.

"You look great," Charli said, which was the truth. Her luminous gray eyes looked bigger, the beautiful shape of her face and neck was more visible now and she looked altogether more sophisticated and…older.

"When did you get this done?"

"This morning. I was coming tomorrow to show you." She bit her lip, her expression suddenly dark and stormy. She took Charli's hand. "Come to my room, okay?"

"What's wrong?" Charli asked after Valentina closed the bedroom door behind them.

"Massimo was furious when I came home this morning," Valentina said, her eyes flashing with anger. "It's my hair! I should be able to do with it what I want!"

Shades of Richard. What was wrong with these men? Why did they feel they had to control everything?

"You'd think I'd committed some crime the way he reacted," Valentina went on. "I just don't get it. He's always giving me these lectures about honesty and integrity and moral values, but I don't understand what my hair has to do with that."

She opened the door to her clothes closet and pulled out a dress. "What do you think of this? I just bought it yesterday." She held it in front of her. "I don't wear dresses much, but I really liked it."

"It's great. I like the color." It was periwinkle-blue and white and looked fresh and cool.

Valentina stared at herself in the mirror, her eyes unfocused. "You know, sometimes I think he's afraid I'm going to become some sort of man-hunting witch, cheating men and lying to get what I want."

Charli laughed. "Why in the world would he think that?"

Valentina shrugged helplessly and tossed the dress on

the bed. "I have no idea. You wouldn't believe what a boring good girl I am. I haven't even had sex yet."

"Wow. And you're already seventeen?"

"Don't laugh at me. I'm probably the only one in my whole school."

"Probably not. And you're smart to wait and you know it."

Valentina sighed. "I know." She sagged down on the side of the bed and frowned. "You know, I don't know of any guy I even want to have sex with."

"Fortunately you have plenty of time to find one."

"And he'd better like my short hair." She ran her hands through it and giggled. "I told Massimo if he didn't shut up about my hair I'd dye half of it orange and the other half purple. You should have seen his face."

Charli could well imagine.

Moments later the man in question stood towering in the doorway and Charli's secret hope not to have to face Massimo vanished. His expression as he looked at her promised nothing good.

"May I have a word with you?" he asked with such cold arrogance she practically shivered.

"Go ahead," she said, trying to look casual.

"In my office."

She clenched her teeth. "Excuse me? Is that an order?"

His eyes narrowed. "In my office, *please*," he said with exaggerated politeness.

She glanced at her watch. "I'm not sure I have time." A lie, but she wasn't going to make this easy for him.

"It will only be a moment."

"That's all I have, much as I would love to stay and chat." She turned and looked at Valentina, giving her a quizzical shrug. "I suppose I'd better find out what crime I have committed. I'll be right back."

She followed him down the hall. "Massimo," she said, taking the initiative as soon as they'd entered his office, "don't tell me this is about Valentina's hair."

"Have a seat," he said, waving at one of the chairs.

"I'm fine, thanks." She frowned at him. "Why are you so upset? It's only hair."

"It's not only hair." Hands resting on his hips, he was standing in the middle of the room, his face expressionless.

She observed him for a moment, understanding dawning. "No, you're right," she said slowly, "it's not only about hair. I think I know what it is, Massimo."

"Really? And what is that?" His imperious expression grated on her nerves.

"You don't like losing control. That's part of it. And the other part is that you don't like what you see when you look at her now. It frightens you."

"Frightens me?" He gave a dry little laugh.

"She looks more grown-up, more sophisticated. Your little sister who always needed your protection is a young woman now who needs some freedom and independence and you don't like it." She paused for effect. "And yes, the men will be looking at her; they already were, I'm sure. She's beautiful, but she will have to learn how to handle the attention. You need to advise her, not try to keep her protected."

"Thank you for the lecture," he said coolly, "but she's my sister and as long as she is my responsibility she must listen to me. And I suggest you try not to influence her and encourage her in ways I do not approve of." The arrogant tone of his voice was infuriating.

"Listen to yourself, Massimo! You sound like some kind of control freak! She's *seventeen* years old and in your opinion she should need big brother's approval about the way she has her hair?'' Anger rushed hot through her blood. ''Are you out of your mind? This is the twenty-first century!''

''And I am responsible for her.''

''Yes, she's still dependent on you as her guardian, but she needs to learn to make independent decisions. What kind of woman do you want her to be? Someone who waits for her husband to make all the decisions? Tell her what to wear, tell her how to have her hair. What to eat in a restaurant? Who to vote for?''

She couldn't stop herself. She saw his face, the surprise in his eyes, yet she raged on about the evils of controlling men and the damage he would cause his sister with his behavior.

''Pretty soon she'll be wearing only what he wants her to wear. Next he'll be telling her what to think and how to behave and not go out with her friends and every time she has an original thought he'll tell her she's being ridiculous or she makes no sense…'' Her voice shook, her eyes burned with tears. ''Don't do this to her, Massimo!''

She stopped herself, could not believe what had come over her. Massimo looked at her silently, his expression unreadable.

She turned on her heel and rushed out of his office, tried to calm herself as she walked back to Valentina's room to get her purse and the clothes she'd left behind.

She had to get away.

Fortunately Valentina was not in her room. Charli gathered her things and fled. She'd call Valentina later.

As she climbed down the stone steps back to town, all she could think of was how lucky she was to have her own apartment. How very happy she was not to have to spend time with Massimo anymore.

* * *

The Piazza di San Bonaventura was an interesting place to watch the world go by. Charli was sitting at the outdoor coffee shop with her mid-morning cappuccino and *sfogliatella* pastry, watching the people, one of her favorite pastimes. Three fashionably dressed young women sat at the next table, smoking, drinking coffee and working their cellphones. Beautiful nails, beautiful hair, beautiful clothes.

It was a glorious day, and she was feeling wonderful. She'd been up early and had worked on her balcony on the laptop for four hours, as was her habit since moving into the apartment, and, as was her habit, she was now sitting here at the outdoor coffee shop soaking up things Italian.

Her cellphone rang and she fished it out of her handbag. "Hello?" she offered.

"Hello, Charli."

Massimo. Her heart lurched on its own accord, which did not please her. Their conversation of a few days ago was still fresh in her mind.

"Hello, Massimo. Did I do something else wrong?"

"I know you do not feel particularly charitable toward me," he said wearily, "but I need your help."

"Really?" she asked coolly. "What's the matter? Did Valentina run away?"

"No," he said, "and she won't be able to for a while."

"What did you do? Lock her up in her room? Afraid she'll dye her hair orange or get a ring through her nose?"

"I didn't hear about the ring through her nose."

"I made that up. But you never know. And then there are the tattoos, of course."

"Thank you, I feel better now. And, to answer your question, no, I have not locked her up in her room. It was not necessary. She managed to get herself imprisoned in

the house without any help from me.'' He paused, probably to give her a moment to consider the meaning of his
words.

They made no sense to her at all.

''If this is a riddle, I don't get it.''

''She broke her leg yesterday. The cast is up to the
middle of her thigh, and—''

''Oh, no, that's terrible!'' Alarm and pity filled her.
She'd never had a broken bone herself, but it sounded
excruciating. ''What happened? Is she all right? Is she in
pain?''

''She will live, she tells me. She's not in a lot of pain,
but she's in a horrible humor—mood. She's not going
back to school next week. For the next six weeks she will
not be roaming far.''

''I'm so sorry. I'll call her. Can I come to see her this
afternoon?''

''Of course. She'll be happy to see you.'' He paused.
''Charli, I need your help.''

An ambulance turned into the piazza, lights flashing,
sirens shrieking. Charli covered her right ear with her
hand.

''Yes, sure, what can I do?''

''Move back here. Keep Valentina company.'' He went
on saying something about Rome and trips, but she didn't
hear it.

Move back into the villa?

Charli stared at the ambulance moving across the piazza, scattering pigeons and pedestrians, shredding the
peace with its siren, warning of danger and disaster.

Somebody besides her was in big trouble.

CHAPTER NINE

"CHARLI? Is that a siren? Did you hear me?"

She swallowed, felt panic rising. "Yes, I heard you." Her voice squeaked with nervousness. She couldn't do it. It was too dangerous to spend time with him in the same place, to see him every day and battle her attraction for him. Massimo was all wrong for her. She couldn't afford to fall for him. The siren shrieked and shrieked. Her head began to pound.

"Valentina is driving me crazy, Charli. I need your help. Please, come back and stay at the house."

The ambulance came to a stop in front of the Santa Lucia Pizzeria and the siren halted in mid-shriek, the abrupt silence almost ominous.

"Yes, yes, of course I'll come," she heard herself say.

From her balcony, an hour later, Charli surveyed the other balconies across the courtyard. On one a young woman watered her plants. On another a dog lay asleep, one leg poking outside the railing. From the open windows of the apartment above came cooking noises—the clattering of pots and pans, water running. She smelled the fragrance of garlic and herbs and tomatoes cooking.

Her lunch plate held fresh bread she'd bought in the *panetteria* on the way back from the coffee shop, provolone cheese, a ripe red tomato, fresh green sage leaves. A yellow bowl of purple grapes was dessert. Together it looked like a colorful painting, a piece of edible art.

From somewhere the voice of a woman called out across the courtyard and another one answered, laughing.

She loved this place, all the life going on for her to observe. Laundry hung out to dry—sheets and old-lady underwear on one balcony, sexy tops and lacy bras on another. Through open windows came the sounds of babies crying, phones ringing, soap opera stars weeping on TV.

Massimo had asked her to come back and stay at the villa and she'd said yes.

She was trying hard not to panic, not to feel that this was a terrible mistake. She knew what frightened her most and it wasn't Massimo. It was herself. She was afraid of her own feelings for him. Afraid of doing something stupid, like falling in love with him.

She thought of Valentina, now confined to the sofa with her leg in a cast and her friends in school again next week. Even Gina, her friend from her elementary school days, would move away. Nothing to do but read and watch TV and do whatever homework the school in Rome would send her.

How could she have possibly said no to Massimo's request?

"Don't you worry I'll be a bad influence on her?" she'd asked him, unable to resist the impulse to put him on the defensive. Not high-minded of her, but there it was. She'd still been sitting on the piazza watching the medics take a man on a stretcher into the ambulance.

"She likes you, Charli," he'd said, "and I want her happy, and I'm sorry I offended you."

Making nice, now that you need me, are you? she'd almost asked, but contained the childish impulse. Surely she owed him a favor in spite of what he'd said to her. He'd helped her when she'd needed help, had rescued her from sleeping in the street when she couldn't get into the apartment.

And Valentina...she'd do a lot for Valentina. She'd already talked to her on the phone, heard the whole sorry tale about how she had made one silly little misstep, tripped and tumbled down a set of marble steps and landed in a most unfortunate bodily position. Her right leg had objected in dramatic fashion. "I heard it crack, Charli!" Valentina had wailed, which wasn't a detail Charli relished thinking about.

In the apartment above the baby cried. Charli heard the soothing sounds of the mother comforting the child. She couldn't hear the words, but the tone of her voice was universal. She'd seen the two on a couple of occasions when they'd gone out for a walk. The baby was picture-perfect cute with huge brown eyes and dark curly hair and a toothless smile that could melt a heart of stone.

She felt a sudden yearning to hold a baby, have one of her own, feel its soft warm weight in her arms. The strength of the feeling surprised her and she grew still, savoring the moment, aware of a delicious sense of freedom: I can have a baby if I want to.

She'd told herself for so long she didn't want children that all those maternal feelings had gone underground. And now, suddenly, here they were again, liberated, joyous.

Richard had had their life together already planned out, with no assistance from her. A plan that included a big house in the suburbs, two children and trips to Europe to get cultured.

She remembered being furious, and frightened. Not because there had been anything wrong with his plan apart from his snobbish desire to get "cultured", but because he'd apparently considered her presence in his life as something he could simply steer and direct. As if she were an appliance with buttons and dials. She'd felt frightened because she'd felt a loss of control.

"I'm not sure I want children at all," she'd said, in an intuitive impulse to resist his controlling attitude. Of course, he'd not taken her seriously. He'd smiled indulgently, taken her in his arms and said that of course she wanted children later.

And so, subconsciously, she'd set out to prove him wrong. She could see that now. She listened to the mother singing a lullaby in Italian, sweet and soothing.

She wanted babies. She wanted a husband. Probably not in that order.

She thought of Massimo, who did not want to marry again. According to Valentina. Why was she thinking about Massimo? Danger signals flashed in her head and she came hastily to her feet. She had to pack some of her things. Massimo was coming to pick her up in his car and take her back to the villa.

She found her old room at the villa filled with the fragrance of flowers. A luxuriant arrangement gloried on a glass-topped table. Blooms of all sorts were gathered together in a stunning combination of colors and sizes— birds of paradise, orchids, roses, lilies and other exotic flowers she could not name.

A small card was tucked inside the greenery, almost hidden.

Please accept these as a token of my gratitude. Grazie mille! Massimo.

"I didn't think you would come," Massimo said to Charli later that evening, wondering why he had admitted his uncertainty to her. She was sitting across from him at the dinner table on the terrace and looked delicious in an apricot-colored shirt, her curls doing a shimmering dance whenever she moved a little, her voice sing-song seduction as she spoke. He didn't want to notice these things, but he did.

"I'm a sucker for the sick and suffering, that's why," she said with a touch of humor. The suffering Valentina had just been helped to her room. She had refused dessert, afraid she was going to grow fat being more or less immobile for the next six weeks or so.

Charli never refused dessert. He watched her as she slipped a spoonful of the creamy *zabaione* into her mouth, noticed how she savored it.

"I want to ask you a question," he said. "About the hair incident."

"You're not still mad about that, are you?" Her blue eyes challenged him.

"No, but I'm curious why *you* were so angry—that was not only about my reaction to Valentina's hair, was it?"

"It wasn't?" She didn't look at him, took another spoonful of *zabaione*.

"It was about you."

She grimaced. "Are you going to play psychoanalyst now?"

"Am I right?"

"Yes. And I apologize for my outburst. This is so delicious, especially with the berries on it. What is it called?"

"You are changing the subject."

She didn't look at him. "So I am."

"So, what happened to you?"

"I used to have long hair, too. Three months ago I cut

it all off.'' She picked up a raspberry with her fingers and put it in her mouth.

He tried to visualize her with long hair but couldn't. He liked her hair the way it was, a halo of soft bouncy curls that forever tempted him to touch, feel the softness around his fingers, against his mouth. He pushed away the treacherous thoughts.

So she'd cut her hair, like Valentina had. A coincidence, maybe. He didn't see the relevance. ''And your big brother was angry?'' he asked in an attempt at humor. She didn't have a big brother.

''No. Richard was. He was the man I was seeing then.''

He felt a jab of hostility at the thought of another man with her. It was a ridiculous emotion he could not allow himself to dwell on. He wiped his mouth with his napkin.

''He liked your long hair, obviously. I can sympathize.''

''What bothered him most was that I didn't ask for his approval first.'' She gave him a meaningful look. ''He had every right not to like my short hair, but he didn't have the right to dictate what I could or could not do with my hair. Or what clothes to wear.''

''He told you what clothes to wear?'' Surely she was not serious. But by the look on her face he knew she was very serious indeed.

''Oh, yes he did. When we went out to a party, he'd always tell me what he thought I'd look good in and what he wanted me to wear. Sometimes he'd even go shopping with me if I needed something dressy for an event.''

She had to be making this up. He couldn't imagine a worse nightmare than to go shopping for clothes with a woman.

She gave him an evil look. ''Don't look at me like that! I know I was an idiot! He was very controlling and some-

how I let myself be pushed around.'' She bit her lip and
looked away, but he caught the shine of tears in her eyes.
It disturbed him to see it.

He felt the light dawning. The things she had said during her outburst made sense to him now.

"How long were you together?" he asked.

He saw her swallow.

"Almost two years." She sucked in a deep breath. "I
should have run after two weeks, but I was crazy in love
with him and then I was in denial. Really pathetic, you
know."

He couldn't for the world see how that was possible.
How a man, any man, had been able to control her, this
woman who clearly had a mind of her own and wasn't
afraid to give voice to her thoughts.

She gave a crooked little smile. "You look surprised,"
she said.

"I hadn't thought of you as someone who lets herself
be pushed around."

"Neither had I until it happened to me," she said dryly.
"Love is blind, as they say. He was a very charming guy
and he had a certain way about him. I don't know." She
hunched a shoulder in a gesture of embarrassment. "I just
was so stupid not to see what was happening. But then
nobody did, except Bree, my best friend. She kept telling
me and telling me, but I wouldn't see it. Nobody else saw
it either because they were all half in love with him too.
Drugged by his charm, like me." She gave a little shud-
der. "I hate to think what would have happened had I
married him."

"So what happened for you to recognize what was going on?"

Her eyes darkened with anger. "Would you believe he
had the gall to forbid me to come here to deal with the

apartment? I was so excited about going to Italy, about the apartment, but he didn't care about any of that. He didn't want me to travel. Mostly he didn't want me to travel without him. He was always talking about going to Europe, but of course it had to be on his terms. My going to Italy wasn't on his terms so he wanted nothing to do with it. Besides, he couldn't take the time off from work at the time and so he demanded I stay at home to cater to him." She sighed, stuck out her lower lip and blew a curl off her forehead. "It was the last straw. I finally saw through him. Or admitted that I did, anyway."

She stopped suddenly, chewed her lower lip. "I'm sorry. I shouldn't have said all that."

"Why not? Wasn't it true?"

"Oh, yes, but it's not cool to talk about former relationships and criticize your ex-partner; I mean, after all, you made the choice to be with him, so what does that say about you?" She grimaced in self-deprecation. "Well, I know what it says about me that I spent two years of my life with Richard, and it's not flattering. I'll claim temporary insanity. And now I really don't want to talk about this anymore." She lifted her glass. "To freedom."

He was a little surprised she did not leave after the coffee, but agreed to a *digestivo*. He poured her a *limoncello* and had a *grappa* himself. Feeling restless, he came to his feet and suggested they check out the view from the edge of the terrace.

"Look, how beautiful," she said, pointing at what must be an enormous yacht all lit up and glittering like a jewel in the dark of the night. "It looks magical."

He watched her smile as she stared at the yacht, her face soft in the moonlight, and it took all his restraint not to reach out to her and touch her.

What was it about her that made him so restless? Surely

it was not just the physical need for a woman. She wasn't gorgeous in any kind of glamorous way. She was not exotic or mysterious or sultry like some women he'd met in his travels.

There was something about Charli that was more appealing than all of that. She was fresh and real. Her laugh was artless, her voice had a sing-song lilt that resonated with something inside him. A yearning for...what?

She was like a fresh spring breeze blowing through the dank dungeons of his emotional life.

There was nothing wrong with his emotional life. He liked it just the way it was.

She glanced sideways at him as if she'd felt his regard. She stood very still, her eyes meeting his.

Then she looked away again, the silence filled with knowing.

He put his empty glass on the wall and jammed his hands into his pockets. "Charli," he said, "I want you to know that I asked you to come back here because of Valentina. Not for my own selfish amorous purposes."

"Of course," she said, no inflection in her voice. He wasn't sure if she was serious or not.

"Which doesn't mean that your presence here doesn't appeal to my selfish amorous instincts." He watched her, seeing her eyes darken.

"Is that a warning?" Her voice was quiet, with a hint of threat.

"No. Just a statement of fact."

"All right, consider me informed."

"I want you. You know that."

She said nothing, clearly feeling no need to respond. He had stated what she already knew, of course.

"But what I also want is for you to be here for

Valentina, so I suppose that if I don't want you running out on us I'll be required to behave like a gentleman.''

She gave a little smile. "As opposed to what? A breast-beating Neanderthal?''

"No,'' he said softly and, against his own plan, he reached out and touched her hair. "As opposed to a lover who wants to make passionate love to you and give you pleasure.''

She was silent and he moved his hand and caressed her cheek, which was soft and warm. "But I'll behave myself. Because I wouldn't want you to think I was controlling and manipulative and forcing you against your will.''

Against her will—that was a laugh. She was putty in his hands and she knew it. Everything about her begged him to continue. She was trembling. And she was fighting it. It would be so easy.

"You're having fun?'' she asked, her tone a mixture of anger and mockery.

He withdrew his hand. "I'm not your Richard.''

He had not known he was going to say that. There was anger in his voice, suddenly. He recognized it himself. He remembered the shine of tears in her eyes.

She lifted her chin. "I didn't say that.''

"No, but that's what you think.''

She took a step back, hands clenched by her side. "Don't you dare tell me what I think!''

"But it's true. You think I'm like him and that's why you are keeping me at a distance, isn't it?''

"What I'm saying is that I don't want an affair,'' she said. "I don't want to be in love! I don't want the complications and, you know what, Massimo? You should respect my wishes and leave me alone!''

He looked at her face, saw the fear hiding behind the anger and felt a primitive impulse to protect and defend.

He wanted to take her into his arms and tell her…tell her what? That she was safe with him? Surely he could make no such promises. He wanted no complications either, no woman to keep forever. He had no love to offer for the long run. The present was all he had to give, and she didn't want it—at least her rational mind told her so, if not her body.

He had no idea what to do and it was not a good feeling. He always knew what to do. In business he had no trouble making decisions, planning, ordering, executing, managing, taking charge.

He did not know what to do with this woman. But touching her now would not be helpful. He shoved his hands once again into his trouser pockets and took a restorative breath, forcing himself to remain calm, to think rationally. Not an easy thing to do under the circumstances.

"I'll leave you alone," he said, hoping somehow he'd be able to. Being a saint wasn't one of his strengths.

"Good!" She started across the terrace toward the door into the house.

"One more thing," he said and she turned to face him, crossing her arms in front of her chest in an instinctive gesture of defense. "If you change your mind, you know where to find me."

She didn't even bother to respond and moved through the doors into the house.

He sighed heavily and turned his gaze back to the view.

Something odd caught his attention. There was a small light on in the old Roman watch-tower clinging to the cliffs. It was always shrouded in darkness. A relic of ancient times, it no longer served a practical purpose. The light moved around, searching. Who was there? Had some crazy tourists climbed the treacherous path in the darkness to spend the night in the watch-tower?

What was there to find in that heap of dead stones? Romance? Adventure?

There had been no life amid those ancient walls for a long time.

Damn, damn! Charli dropped herself flat on her bed and pummeled the pillow. She couldn't stand it. She'd made a mistake. She should never have come. One moment Massimo was nice and courteous, the next he was making her so furious.

Furious. Was that really what she was?

I don't want to be in love. Her own words echoed in her head like a warning. She was furious with herself, furious because she didn't want to be in love and she was afraid she was already halfway there. She pushed her face into the pillow and groaned. More than halfway.

She couldn't stand this, couldn't stand thinking about it. She sat up.

She should check up on Valentina. See if she needed anything else, something to drink, a pain pill maybe.

Valentina lay in bed reading a fashion magazine, her leg propped up high on a stack of pillows.

"I hate this," she said. "I hate sleeping on my back."

"Are you hurting?"

"No. It doesn't hurt much at all. Weird, isn't it?"

"It seems like it, yes."

Valentina sighed and glanced down at the magazine, then back up at Charli. "I forgot to tell you—Massimo told me he was sorry he was angry with me for cutting my hair."

"Really? When was that? Just now?"

"No, no, before I broke my leg. After you left that time you came here to get your things."

Days ago, when she'd lost it and spilled her own frustrations. "I see. I'm glad." She grinned. "See, he's not so hopeless after all."

Valentina rolled her eyes. "We'll see."

Charli wished Valentina goodnight and went back to her room to get ready for the night.

She lay in bed, thinking about the evening and bits and pieces of the conversation floated through her mind like balloons in the sky.

I hadn't thought of you as someone who lets herself be pushed around.

I'm not your Richard.

Massimo told me he was sorry he was angry with me for cutting my hair.

She'd watched Massimo tend to his sister with love and care, ready to do anything in his power to make her more comfortable, wanting her not to be so miserable.

Was she overreacting? Was he not the authoritarian controlling type she was making him out to be in her mind?

If you change your mind, you know where to find me.

Charli stood in her little apartment kitchen and couldn't believe what had been accomplished in a mere three weeks. Lovely new Italian tiles hugged the walls above a new countertop. New cabinets, a new stove and refrigerator gave the small place a fresh, clean look. The terracotta floor had been restored to its original warm red color. The other walls were freshly whitewashed, the woodwork painted.

She was in love with this kitchen and it was hers.

Massimo stood leaning in the doorway, watching her. "You're happy with it?"

"It's wonderful." She gave him a considering look. "And I have no illusions about why it was all done so quickly, efficiently and beautifully."

"It's all about contacts, knowing the right people."

And Massimo had the contacts in this town and knew the right people. He had given her names, made calls for her. And possibly he'd made behind-the-scenes calls as well, she didn't know, but the job had been done and done well and she was happy. And they'd already started work on the bathroom as well. Her inherited euro bank account would be depleted when she was done, but she'd have herself a great little place in Italy. She'd rent it out when possible, and spend time when she could.

"Thank you," she said, meaning it, smiling at him. Surely it wasn't so terrible to accept this sort of practical help? She had to stop being oversensitive. Really, she was working on it.

Fortunately Massimo spent most of the work week in his office in Rome, driving back to the villa for long weekends. He'd flown to New York once on business, and this past week he'd been in Morocco for a few days. Not having him around every single day gave her nervous system a rest, but to her annoyance her nights were often full of dreams of him.

While he was away, she'd been keeping Valentina company. She wasn't the easiest of patients, and was sometimes in tears feeling sorry for herself. She wanted to go back to school, to her friends, but the school's old building with its many levels and stairs and spread-out campus was almost impossible to negotiate even with crutches.

"May I see the rest of the place?" Massimo asked.

It seemed strange to think he hadn't been inside the

apartment at all, so she gave him the tour, which took approximately ten minutes with her talking stretching the time. With Antonia's help, she told him, she'd gotten rid of most of the old-fashioned furniture, and no, they were not antique treasures, she'd checked. But she had kept much of the linens—lovely linen sheets and tablecloths embroidered by loving hands and soft from much use and washing. And she'd found a couple of nice old things among the dishes and knick-knacks, and she'd let Antonia take whatever she wanted, which wasn't much, because most of the things were the simple possessions of ordinary people, not of value, and mostly just old and worn.

Okay, she was talking too much, about girlie things no less, but she'd had fun and in the end Antonia had been such a help and Charli had so enjoyed her company.

They were back in the kitchen and she pointed at the open door. "And here's the balcony. My introduction to Italian life."

He curved his mouth in a half-smile. "A noisy one, I'm sure." And, as if to prove it, a dog began to bark furiously in the courtyard below.

She stepped outside and he followed her and glanced around at the view of open windows and balconies with their potted plants and washing lines and the dog with his paw poking out through the railing.

"Have a seat." Charli indicated one of the wrought-iron chairs flanking the round marble-topped table. "Would you care for a glass of *frizzante*?"

She was the hostess now, and she liked the feeling of being in her own space, but in this space was Massimo and it made her oddly nervous.

Being standoffish and staying out of his way was easier than playing the hostess, thanking him for his help and generally trying to be gracious. The dynamic was changing. He'd been the perfect gentleman, as he had promised, the past few weekends. Which was not to say that the atmosphere had been calm and serene between them.

He'd be happy with a glass of *frizzante*, he said and lowered himself on to one of the chairs and stretched out his long legs.

The Duomo bells chimed out the time—four quick ones for the hour and three slow ones for the quarter hours. Four-forty-five. She loved the sound of it, the ambience it created.

She brought the bottles and glasses to the balcony and he unscrewed the caps of both the bottles. He had beautiful hands with strong lean fingers that moved quickly and competently. Her heart skittered a little as she watched him—and it was disturbing to notice how little it took for her to feel a reaction when she was with him. Every cell was always aware of him, alive with an energy that was impossible to ignore.

She took her glass and drank from the cold, fizzy wine. In the apartment above, the baby began to cry, apparently just waking up from her nap. She listened for a moment as the mother comforted the baby, then became aware of Massimo watching her.

''Why are you looking at me like that?''

He gave an amused little smile. ''You were listening to that baby and your maternal instincts were in full swing all over your face.''

She gave a little shrug. ''Well, what can I say? I'm blessed with female hormones.''

''You want children?'' It was a casual question.

''Yes, when the time is right. I think I'd like a husband to be part of the scenario.''

''So this Richard didn't sour the idea of marriage for you?''

She shook her head. "No. It just made me more care-ful." She felt nervous suddenly. "I mean, I don't want to marry the wrong man, and—" She stopped. She wasn't making this any better. He probably thought she'd been pushing him away because she considered him not good husband material, but then he wasn't, was he? "What about you?" she said quickly. "I suppose you're not in-terested in having children. I understand you don't want to marry again."

He'd never mentioned it himself, but she supposed the information wasn't much of a secret, and living in a household with two women who'd known him for years and years it should not surprise him that the word was out.

He arched his brow. "Women always talk too much," he said mildly.

"How long were you married?" she ventured.

"Three years. And no, I'm not planning to marry again." She caught something dark and desperate in his eyes.

"Do you miss her?" she asked.

"It's been a long time." He put his glass on the table and stood up. "We'd better get going."

She stood up, too. They faced each other on the small balcony.

"Why don't you want to talk about her?" she asked, amazing herself by asking the question about a subject so sensitive. Yet she wanted to know.

His face grew hard. "What would you like me to say?"

She shrugged, trying to remember what Valentina had said. "I don't know…that she was beautiful, that you loved her, that you planned to have children and…you know, the regular stuff people say."

"All right. All that." His voice was hard and cold.

"She was beautiful. I loved her. We planned—" He stopped himself, made a dismissive gesture. "What the hell use is this? It's over. It's done."

Her heart was beating fast. It disturbed her to see the anger in his eyes, the hard set of his chin.

"Why are you so angry?" And as she heard herself ask the question she wondered if she were stupid or dense. He was angry because fate had taken his wife from him, the wife he had loved. It was a normal reaction, wasn't it? It was one more reason not to get involved with him— she didn't want to have to compete with a dead wife.

"I'm not angry." His voice was cold and controlled, the heat suddenly suppressed. His face was expressionless.

An uneasy doubt wriggled in her mind. Something wasn't right, but she had no idea what it was.

He moved abruptly. "Let's go."

She picked up the bottles and glasses and followed him inside.

That night Charli dreamed of a baby, of Massimo looking angry, telling her he didn't want any babies and that she should stop asking questions.

She awoke, feeling the wetness of tears on her cheeks. She stared at the ceiling, recalling the dream. How strange.

She felt a sudden deep yearning to know him better. To see what sadness lay hidden behind that anger in his eyes—eyes dark and deep as a wintry sea. What wrecks lay below the stormy surface? What treasures lost?

And for a fleeting moment she wondered what would happen if she got up and opened the door, walked down the hall and went into the room where Massimo lay sleeping.

What would he say if she slipped into his bed and told him, Please, Massimo, I don't want you to be unhappy.

He'd make love to her, that was what would happen. And that was all that would happen because Massimo wasn't giving his heart away again. She shouldn't have any illusions.

CHAPTER TEN

IT WAS a gorgeous late-summer evening in Rome, the ancient buildings washed in the golden light of the setting sun. Massimo crossed the Corso Rinascimento and strode toward home. The company office was a mere ten-minute walk from his city-center apartment and the walk did him good. He was working harder than normal these days, in an effort to keep Charli out of his thoughts, which appeared to be a losing battle. He'd decided that he'd wait for her to change her mind about having an affair, but waiting wasn't something he did well. Patience was not one of his virtues.

The cellphone in his pocket started to ring and he reached for it as irritation swept over him. He'd had a long stressful day and he wanted to be left alone. The display read Valentina's number and he flipped open the phone. "*Pronto*," he said.

Valentina's excited voice rushed into his ear like a waterfall, begging him, *please*, would he collect Melissa from school and bring her home to the villa for the weekend?

It was a terrible idea. It was a great idea.

Why had he not thought of it? Guilt softened his annoyance. Valentina needed her friends, and most of them were right here in school in Rome. Having Melissa staying for the weekend was a small price to pay for Valentina's happiness.

He turned a corner, moved around two double-parked cars and passed a flower shop. He smelled the sweet scent of roses and Charli's smile flashed through his mind. He took a deep breath and tried to focus on Valentina's voice trying to persuade him.

"She has permission from her parents and you'll have to sign a paper or something," Valentina was saying, trying to make sure he knew all obstacles had been considered and conquered and all he had to do was pick her up.

"All right," he heard himself say. "I'll call the school and tell them what time I'll collect her."

Flipping his phone shut, he narrowly missed stepping on a tiny dog on a leash. The bejeweled matron holding the leash gave him an evil look out of heavily made-up eyes.

He crossed the street and entered the ancient *palazzo* where his apartment was located. He greeted the *portinaia* and took the lift to the top floor. Blessed quietude greeted him as he opened the ornately carved wooden door to his residence. No pop music throbbed in the air, no women of any sort rushed out to demand his attention.

He was exhausted.

He took off his tie and jacket, poured himself a glass of San Pellegrino and sat down in his favorite chair. He glanced at his watch. He had an hour before he'd meet the Argentinians at the restaurant. He didn't normally go home before going out to dinner, usually did the customary thing and spent time with friends in a bar before eating, but he'd had a hellish day and he'd been around people every minute of it and he wanted a little solitude.

He picked up the remote and turned on some quiet jazz. He drank his mineral water and studied the large painting on the wall across the room. The serene dark eyes of an Asian beauty looked back at him. Dressed in a traditional costume of some ethnic minority, the young woman sat straight and poised, looking calmly ahead, her delicate hands folded in her lap. He had acquired the painting in Myanmar and it had cost him a small fortune. It was exquisite. The girl's face was flawless, her hair smoothed back shiny and glossy as silk, not a hair out of order. He'd been enchanted by the painting, yet there had always been something about it that had niggled at his awareness and he'd never been able to pinpoint what it was.

He sighed and closed his eyes.

And what he saw in his mind's eye was Charli.

He opened his eyes. He knew exactly what was wrong with the painting.

The problem was that there was *nothing* wrong with the painting. Nothing wrong with the skill and talent of the artist. Nothing wrong with the serene beauty.

It was all *too* perfect.

What he wished he were looking at right now was Charli. Charli with the freckles on her nose, her bouncy curls free and unrestrained, her generous smiling mouth, a little too large for her face, her eyes that sometimes were not serene at all, but stormy with emotion.

He came to his feet, restless, and moved through the rooms, looking at all the art he had collected over the years, taken home from his travels to exotic places—paintings and wood carvings and sculptures and handmade rugs; and he wondered what Charli would think of them. Damn, he was thinking of her too much. And he'd be home for the weekend again and it would be hell keeping his amorous impulses under control. All he wanted when she was anywhere in the neighborhood was to haul her into his arms, bury his face in her hair, press her against him and let the passion take over.

He was an idiot. With a woman like Charli, he knew where this would lead and he didn't want to go even near it. What the hell was wrong with him? He wanted no emotional entanglements, for God's sake.

He finished his water, paced around the house, stopped in front of the window and stared unseeingly down into the narrow street below.

He turned. Put his glass down. Picked up the phone. Called Charli's number.

"*Pronto*," she said, answering like a true Italian.

"Just checking you haven't run away," he said.

She laughed. "Why would I do that?"

"My sweet sister might have driven you to it."

"Not at all. I'm trying to keep her entertained. She's teaching me Italian, which she finds quite a hilarious enterprise."

"Let's hope she's teaching you something you can use in polite company," he said with a voice full of doom.

"It's a risk I'm aware of. Let's check it out. Ask me something."

"Would you like to go out to dinner with me on Saturday night?" he said promptly.

"Oh," she said, surprised. "I mean, in Italian."

He repeated the question in Italian.

"*Non capisco*," she said, not missing a beat and he laughed.

"You understand perfectly."

She chuckled. "So how's my Italian?"

"Very good. You can even *lie* in Italian."

"I'm so proud of myself," she said dryly. "Oh, by the way, Valentina tells me you are bringing her friend Melissa to spend the weekend. She's so happy."

"Good. And while they watch those horrid movies Melissa will no doubt bring along and talk about whatever teenagers talk about, we could escape and have dinner out on Saturday night."

There was a pause and he wondered if she might turn him down, convinced he was just like that *maiale*, that swine, Richard. The thought caused a flash of anger and he pushed it aside.

"Thank you, I'd like that," she said then, and to his surprise it sounded as if she meant it.

Charli hunted through the closet for something to wear. She had a date with Massimo, which seemed odd, having been in his house for weeks now and having had dinner with him for many nights.

But this time they were going out and they'd be alone.

She felt a little nervous about it, which seemed ridiculous, especially since they'd be in a public place where he'd hardly have a chance to seduce her. Then again, he'd made no such attempts lately, so what was she worried about?

You know what you're worried about, a little voice said in her head. You're scared because this man is making you feel things you've never felt before.

She pulled out a blue-green silk dress and held it in front of her. It looked cheerful, cool and summery, perfect for a warm Italian evening.

A romantic evening with a sexy Italian. She groaned in frustration at her own thought and slipped the dress on over her head.

She'd been thinking about him too much, wondering about his life, his feelings. Wondering why he had been so angry the time she'd asked about his wife.

She smoothed the fabric over her hips and looked in the mirror.

She was curious, that was all.

Oh, sure, said the little voice.

She slipped on her sandals, picked up her handbag and

went in search of Massimo. He was in the living room waiting for her.

"We'll take the car," he stated. "Unless, of course, you prefer to walk," he added quickly.

Charli glanced down at her high-heeled sandals and considered the options. "If I tried walking down the hill in these you might well end up with two women with broken legs in your house."

"The car it is," he said and she laughed.

He took her to his favorite eatery in town, a small cozy restaurant hidden away in a tiny arched alley. He told her he knew the chef, had gone to school with him as a young boy.

"I would never have found this on my own," Charli said as he held the door open for her. "This town is amazing. It's full of nooks and crannies. I keep discovering new places every time I walk around."

They were seated at a table in the small courtyard and ordered wine. Potted palms and flowering bushes created a garden ambience and the soft light of many candles added romance. Languid guitar music drifted through the warm evening air.

"The owner is his own chef," Massimo explained. "He'll be here in a moment and discuss what he has available and what our choices are. Don't worry, the food is always excellent."

She laughed. "I am not going to worry about food here, believe me. You decide and I'll eat."

"You want me to decide what you should eat?" He sounded surprised.

"Why not? You're the Italian here and I trust your food choices."

"I thought you got away from that Richard because he was deciding everything for you."

She stared at him, digesting his comment. "This is not the same thing. I'm asking you to do it. You're not telling me what to eat because you want to impose your choices on me."

He nodded. "You're right. I wouldn't dream of imposing my choices on you."

"Good," she said, thinking he most surely was imposing his choices on his sister, but deciding it was better not to bring that up.

A handsome man dressed in blinding white appeared at the table, all smiles and charm. Massimo introduced him as Paolo, the owner and chef.

The two men briefly discussed family and friends, and then Paolo described the various marvels he'd be able to create for them this evening, which included *cozze ripiene*, stuffed mussels, and *fagiano arrosto*, roast pheasant, both favorites of Massimo's.

And of course the food was excellent, and Paolo was charming when she asked him questions about the dishes served and he spent quite a bit of time at their table.

"You found yourself an admirer," Massimo said as Paolo retreated to the kitchen after serving them their *secondi*.

She gave a casual little shrug. Did he think she was naive? "He's married. I'm only interested in his cooking. Besides, I assume he flirts with all his female clients. Good for business." Taking knife and fork, she eagerly began to eat her roasted pheasant. She'd never had pheasant before.

"Oh, this is so good," she said after taking the first bite. "I never understand people who are afraid to try what they've never had before." Memories stirred and she caught herself smiling. "My mother is a terrible cook. Maybe that's why I got adventurous, out of self-defense."

"You've had a deprived childhood, then."

She grinned. "Yeah, lots of love, lots of fun, lots of terrible food."

"What about your brother? Is he interested in food now?"

"Ryan? Oh, he's hopeless. He forgets to eat. And if he does eat, it's take-out or something frozen he can heat up in the microwave."

"You said he was still at university. What does he study?"

"Physics. He's a real science nut. His hair is rather wild and wavy because he forgets to get it cut. He has no time for that either because all he does is study and work on research projects. They call him Ryanstein."

He laughed and asked more questions, and she wondered why he suddenly wanted to know more about her background. Maybe he was just making conversation. Anyway, she was happy to sit here in the warm summer night telling him the stories of her life if that was what he wanted to hear.

Then he started talking about Valentina, saying that he had overheard her saying to Melissa that he was unbending in his resolve to send her to university in England.

"I know you think I'm too controlling with Valentina," he said, "and you were right about my reaction to her hair. It was…how do you say? Over the top."

She nodded helpfully. "Over the top."

"And what you said was true. It does frighten me to see her growing up, to see her looking so…like a woman."

"A woman the men would go after." She decided she might as well say it clearly.

"She's only seventeen," he said. "These days at seventeen… I don't want to think about it."

"You'll *have* to think about it. And seventeen isn't twelve, Massimo." In his mind that was probably what she still was.

He stared down at his plate. "I don't want her to get hurt. She's had a lot of hurt already with our parents dying when she was so young. I just want her to be happy, get herself a decent education and find a good man to love and cherish her when she's older."

"But you can't protect her forever, Massimo."

He sighed wearily. "I know."

She put her knife and fork down, leaned forward a little and looked straight at him.

"She's smart, Massimo. I talk to her about boys and sex and all that stuff and she's fine. She will be fine."

He reached out and took her hand. "I want you to know how much I appreciate that you're staying with her. I know it was a big favor to ask you, but—"

"It's all right, Massimo. I like Valentina, you know that. Being with her is sort of like being with the younger sister I never had."

Dessert arrived and he let go of her hand, and she wished he hadn't. The lemon cake was a piece of art as it lay displayed on the plate, a green sprig of mint a contrasting garnish.

Slowly she savored the first bite. "So, you worry about Valentina's future, but tell me, what do you want for yourself in the future?" She surprised herself. The question somehow had popped out.

He looked a bit surprised too, then frowned, as if he'd never considered the question. He answered by telling her about the plans he had for the company, and she listened with attention, taking small bites from her dessert. It was interesting enough, but not what she'd intended as an answer.

"Actually," she said, "I was wondering about your personal life. How do you see your future?"

"I don't think about it." His tone was expressionless.

"How can you not think about it?"

"It's easy. I have lots of other things to think about."

"Don't you have any idea what you'd like your life to be like in ten years or twenty? Nothing to hope for, nothing to look forward to?" How could anyone live that way?

"Hopefully I'll still have money in the bank and won't be languishing in jail." His tone was dry.

"That's pretty impressive all right." Her voice mocked him. "When my dreams include the wish not to be in jail, I'll know I have arrived." She paused. "I do hope you're not one of those companies with crooked executives and crooked bookkeeping?"

He laughed. "Not to worry."

"So, you hope not to be in jail and still have money in the bank. It's a vision of sorts, I suppose. Do you see yourself living alone? With one woman? Or just flitting from one relationship to another?"

He grimaced in distaste, clearly not enthralled by the scenarios she'd brought up. "I was hoping you'd given up on the subject."

She put her spoon down. "No. I want to know what you think." She couldn't believe she had the nerve to be so persistent when it was obvious he wanted the subject dropped.

He shrugged. "I try to live in the moment."

"But you plan for your business, make projections, set goals."

"Yes. However, in my personal life this has not proved to be a successful strategy."

She pushed her plate away, folded her arms on the table

and leaned forward. "You don't want to talk about this, do you?" she asked softly.

"No."

The word hung in the silence between them and she felt suddenly oddly nervous. She hesitated. "So, a few weeks ago, when you said you wanted me, you were strictly talking about living-in-the-moment stuff?"

He met her eyes. "That's all I know how to do."

She held his gaze. "And when it's over, it's over." It was a statement, not a question, because, of course, she already knew.

"Yes, it is, Charli."

The breeze felt cool on her face. Wrapped in her kimono, Charli sat curled up in the wide window seat in her bedroom and stared out over the dark sea, taking a deep breath, smelling the salty water.

Too wound up and restless, she'd lain awake for more than an hour and she couldn't stand being in bed any longer. It had been a wonderful evening. The romantic restaurant, the delicious food and Massimo sitting across from her—it had all been magical. Now all she could think about was Massimo and that she wasn't just attracted to him in a superficial physical, sexual way—she was falling in love with him in a big way.

And falling in love with Massimo was not a good thing.

All this past week, ever since his angry words on her apartment balcony, she'd been thinking and wondering. And what she had realized tonight was that Massimo was afraid to think about the future.

Afraid. Surely he did not seem like a man afraid of anything, yet she'd sensed it on some intuitive level. He lived in the moment. *That's all I know how to do,* he'd said.

Coffee had arrived and she'd dropped the subject.

After dinner, they'd walked through town to the water's edge and strolled along the palm-lined promenade, somehow reluctant to go home to two teenage girls. Crossing a street, he'd taken her hand, a protective gesture that had touched her. She'd not pulled away and they'd held hands for the rest of their walk. It had seemed right. It had felt good. Everywhere in town young couples had walked hand in hand, or sat on benches, kissing passionately. *Amore* everywhere. Italians were affectionate, amorous people and clearly had no problem showing it to the world.

She thought about what he had said. That he was worried about his sister. And that he made no plans for the future because he didn't know how. That when he said he wanted her it had nothing to do with the future. It would be a temporary thing.

At least she knew exactly where she stood with him.

Arriving home after their walk through town, she had thanked him for the dinner and spontaneously stood on tiptoe and kissed him on the cheek—a gesture that had somehow seemed right at the moment. She'd immediately withdrawn, wished him *buona notte* and gone to her room.

The night air was cool and breezy and she loved sitting here with the window open. Movement caught her eye. To her left, part of the terrace was visible and Massimo was out there, standing at the wall, looking out into the night, awake as she was. He was barefoot, wearing jeans only, as if he'd hastily put them on. His broad back and wide shoulders gleamed in the moonlight and she felt heat throbbing through her. He was a beautiful man standing there so quietly in the night. Thinking about what? she wondered. About a future he didn't dare dream about?

He must have sensed something because suddenly he

turned, looked toward her room and saw her at the window.

For a moment he stood very still, looking at her. Then he slowly lifted his hand in greeting. With a little wave she acknowledged his gesture, then she drew back and slipped off the window seat.

Her heart racing, she crossed the room. Don't think, she told herself. Don't think. Go to him. She opened the door quietly and found her way along the dark corridor. The marble was cool on her feet. No sound came from Valentina's room. The girls must have finally fallen asleep.

What if I'm wrong? What if I'm making a terrible mistake?

She rushed across the living room, her bare feet on soft silk rugs. The large glass doors stood open.

Massimo was still standing at the wall, tall and lean and utterly male. She moved across the terrace toward him and nothing now could make her go back. He turned his head when he heard her.

"Can't sleep?" he asked as she came to stand next to him.

The deep timbre of his voice slid through her blood like rich red wine. She shook her head. "No."

They were silent. She was aware of her pulse throbbing, of the vibrations between them.

"You look so beautiful in the moonlight," he said softly, his dark gaze caressing her face. No man had ever looked at her quite like that. Was it the Italian in him? Did it matter?

"Moonlight magic," she said lightly. She wasn't beautiful, had no illusions about that. Certainly not as beautiful as the gorgeous Giulia. Now why had that thought popped into her head? She did not want to think about Giulia. This was not the time.

"You believe in magic?" he asked, smiling a little.

"Yes," she heard herself say, not knowing why she said it so convincingly. She didn't know much about magic, but surely not to believe in it would devalue this moment.

His eyes were dark and full of shadows. "It is very difficult for me not to touch you. Not to kiss you."

The air throbbed between them with a sweet tension. She said nothing, just looked at him with her pulse racing.

"It is not such a good idea for you to be here, Charli." His voice was very low.

She swallowed. "I want to be here." And she did, more than anything. Against all her own good judgment, she wanted to be here with him.

He touched her hair, twirled a curl around his finger. "You're playing dangerous games with me."

She was inches away from his naked chest, longed to put her cheek against the warm skin, feel his heart beating. "Yes, I know I am."

He was silent for a moment as if considering what to reply to what she had just said.

"You told me you're not interested in an affair," he said carefully. "That you don't like controlling men." He gently straightened the curl between his fingers, holding it out from her head.

"I'm not going to allow you to control me." Oh, how brave she sounded. How terrified she was.

Dark shadows danced in his eyes. "I don't *want* to control you, Charli. I *never* wanted to control you." He released the curl and she felt it coil back into its natural shape against her ear. "All I've wanted is to make love to you."

"Why?"

He laughed softly. "What kind of question is that?" He trailed his finger from her temple across her cheek in a featherlike caress. "Because you stir up my fantasies with your smile. Because your eyes are blue as the sky and make me feel like flying." He traced his finger around her mouth. "Because you have beautiful lips made for kissing."

How very poetic. If an American had said those words she would have laughed. She did not feel like laughing. She felt a deep, wondrous thrill of desire.

"I like the way you enjoy your food," he went on. "I like the way you are with my sister and you don't think she's a nuisance. I like that you are charmed by this little old town, that you've made friends with an old housekeeper without even speaking the same language." He paused. "*Ti penso sempre*," he added softly.

I always think of you.

"But you stopped trying to seduce me." She sounded a little breathless, which was not surprising. His touch, barely noticeable, was setting her on fire.

He gave a crooked little smile and dropped his hand away from her face. "Believe me, it's not easy. Not at all a natural thing to do for an Italian."

"So why did you?"

"Because that's what you said you wanted."

A simple answer. A simple truth. She *had* asked him to. And he had obliged. He had not forced his will on her, and how easy it would have been for him to get her into bed with him. He'd known that, surely, yet he hadn't. Something warm and light began to glow inside her.

"Maybe I was wrong," she whispered.

He took her face in his hands, very tenderly. "Do you know what you are doing, *cara*?" he asked gently.

"Yes. It's called living in the moment."

"Charli…" hesitation in his voice. "I don't want to hurt you. I can make no promises."

"I know that." *When it's over, it's over.* She swallowed, wanting to say the words, knowing it was like leaping into dangerous uncertainty, yet wanting to do it anyway. She closed her eyes and lifted her mouth to his.

"When it's over, it's over," she whispered against his lips.

CHAPTER ELEVEN

IN ANSWER, he softly stroked his lips over hers, then eased into a heart-thrilling kiss that was pure seduction. She opened herself to the sensation, feeling the intoxicating heat spreading through her body like smooth, golden cognac. How could he do this with just his mouth, the stroking of his tongue? He took his time, kissing her with exquisite perfection, as if performing a dance to erotic music that went on and on in his head.

She responded to his kiss, answering a need of her own to join in the dance, feeling shivers of sweet desire curling through her.

Finally he lifted his face away from hers and slipped his hands down to her shoulders, skimmed over her breasts with barely a touch and came to rest on the belt tied around her waist.

His eyes locked with hers. ''You're not wearing a nightdress under there.''

''No.'' She swallowed. ''I...never wear any.'' She liked feeling her skin against cool, smooth sheets.

''Ah, a sensualist.'' He loosened the knot of the belt, his eyes still gazing into hers. ''I want to see you,'' he said huskily.

Her breath caught as she felt him slide the kimono off, his hands caressing her arms. The silky fabric slipped down her body and pooled around her feet. She stood naked in front of him, her heart racing, her legs trembling.

He stroked her cheek, then feathered both hands down her throat and across her breasts, then trailed down her waist and hips, exploring her shape. Moving up again, he cupped her breasts, letting their weight rest in the warmth of his hands while brushing his thumbs over her nipples.

"How beautiful you are," he said softly.

The slow heat of arousal simmered in her blood. "Say it in Italian," she whispered, and saw his answering smile.

"*Come sei bella*," he said, and it sounded like music. He bent his head and kissed her breasts, first one then the other, his tongue gently stroking her already eager nipples. She shivered as the sparks of electricity skittered through her bloodstream and rested her hands on his shoulders to steady herself.

"I think we should go inside," she said, suddenly feeling a bit too naked and too exposed out in the open on the terrace. "What if the girls wake up?"

He straightened to look down into her eyes again. "I suppose you're right." A cool waft of air stirred the tousled lock of hair that had fallen across his forehead. She slid her hands down over his chest, feeling the tickle of hair against her palms.

"I want to see you too, Massimo."

He gave a crooked smile. "Fair is fair." He bent down, picked up her robe and draped it over her shoulders. Then he lifted her up in his arms as if she weighed nothing and carried her into the house. She wrapped her arms around his neck, reveling in the sensation of being carried as if she were something precious that needed protection.

His bedroom was bathed in moonlight and the curtainless windows offered a view of the dark Mediterranean.

"No one can see us here," he said as he lay her on the big bed. He went back to the door and locked it, but did not remove the key. "Just in case."

Approaching the bed again, he reached for the zipper of his jeans. No belt.

No shorts, either, she realized as he lowered the zipper and stepped out of the jeans and tossed them on a nearby chair. Her mouth went dry at the sight of him, all bronze naked male desire. He took her breath away and she stared at him, feeling desire flare higher and hotter.

"You *have* seen a naked man before?" he asked, his tone amused.

She tried to find her voice. "I don't remember."

"Good." He lay down next to her on the bed and she shifted a little to give him room. He turned on his side and drew her against him and she sighed as she felt every inch of her warmed by the long length of him, felt the heat of his erection against her body.

Her face lay nestled in the crook of his neck and she breathed in the scent of him, his closeness thrilling her senses, making her feel heady.

"How does this feel?" he asked. "Skin against skin."

"Wonderful," she whispered, loving his voice, his care, his attention.

"Tell me what you like." His fingers began a slow, sexy dance along her neck and back.

"I...I don't know. What do you mean?"

He gave a low chuckle. "Do you have preferences, certain things you find especially pleasurable in lovemaking? I will do what you like."

"Oh." She felt like a total idiot. "No...I mean—" She stopped. Her brain was mush. She couldn't think. "I don't know," she said helplessly.

He tilted his head to the side and cocked an eyebrow. "You don't know what pleases you in bed?"

She swallowed. "I've never been asked that question before. I don't know the lingo."

"Ah," he said softly. "You poor woman. You've never

been properly made love to. I'll have to do something about that.''

She was probably quite deprived in the sex department, she decided, realizing that a self-absorbed control freak like Richard couldn't possibly have been a natural talent in bed. Not like this man, who seemed to want to play with her as if he had all the time in the world.

Problem was that she wasn't sure if she had all the time in the world. His hands were setting her on fire. She stirred restlessly, wanting more. Not that she had the lingo to express exactly what and how. He was stroking her body in the most erotic tantalizing way, finding sensitive places she hadn't known she had, promising delights yet to come. Like reading an expensive menu in a foreign language.

''You do what you think I'll like,'' she said a little breathlessly. ''You're the Italian and I trust your judgment.''

Even in the semi-darkness she could see the laughter flashing in his eyes. ''Are you sure? I wouldn't want you to think I force my preferences—''

''*Shh*,'' she said, tugging his face down to hers again. ''Make love to me. Show me how it's done Italian style.''

''*Si, signorina.*''

And he began to show her in exquisite detail, evoking in her the desire to respond with a passion of her own, to give him back in kind. She loved the muscled hardness of his body, and the way the warm skin felt under her hands and mouth. He tasted of passion and desire, of things forbidden and secret. She reveled in the sound of his ragged breathing, the soft growl of need as he responded to her touch. And on the fringes of her consciousness she was aware of never having experienced such utter, intoxicating pleasure.

And Massimo was giving it to her with generosity and skill, attentive to her needs, taking pleasure from her pleasure.

Her own passion surprised her—the wild abandon as she moved her body with his, only feeling and breathing and sensing. And, as the tension grew, his kisses and caresses grew more erotic, deeper, faster, his lips and fingers exquisite torture, until the feverish hungering inside her became unbearable.

She tugged at his shoulders, raised her hips to him. "Please," she whispered. "I can't—" The feeling of him sliding inside her was pure agonizing ecstasy. Then he began to move and every last remnant of sane thought left her mind. She wanted, ached, needed—primitive desires overwhelming all reason. She arched against him, gripping his hips, wanting him deeper, deeper.

There was only Massimo, their glorious lovemaking and the pure magic of it all as they clung together until the tension shattered, spinning them together into blissful release.

Heart pounding, skin damp, Charli lay spent in Massimo's arms. Delicious languor stole over her and she closed her eyes. She was glad he said nothing and was just holding her. It felt perfect just like this. She sighed. Perfect.

"I talked to your mom the other day," Bree said over the phone. "She's getting excited about the party. Thirty years of marriage, I can't believe it."

Charli had called Bree because it was her birthday, and a phone call was more personal than an e-mail card. In Italy it was almost midnight and the sky was full of stars. Massimo had gone inside to find another bottle of wine and she'd taken the opportunity to call Bree.

"Can you imagine," Bree said, "being married to the same man for all that time and still like him, let alone *sleep* with him?"

Actually, yes, Charli could well imagine it. One week of bliss with Massimo and she had no trouble imagining it at all, but it was a forbidden thought, so to speak.

She didn't really want to discuss happy thirty-year marriages, even though her own parents were the lucky ducks to have one. She glanced up at the moon, which hung full and ripe in the night sky.

Thirty years was the future. Next year was the future. She didn't *do* future these days. She was living purely in the present.

"I don't think about it," she said, which wasn't exactly the truth. She just wished it were the truth. It was difficult not to think and dream of the forbidden.

"What about Massimo?" Bree asked. "Doesn't he inspire dreams of thirty years of marital bliss? Or is this affair merely present-time lust? You're not very revealing in those e-mails of yours, you know."

The subject of their discussion strolled on to the terrace with two glasses of wine. Charli watched him, enjoying the sight of him, the easy way he moved his body. He was the most beautiful man she had ever known. He placed the glasses on the rock wall and sat down next to Charli on the bench. He planted a soft, silent kiss on the corner of her mouth and looked at her with eyes full of smoldering desire. The man had plans. Charli closed her eyes against all that blatant seduction and concentrated on the conversation. No, she hadn't told Bree much about her love-life with Massimo.

Bree was her best friend, but the more intimate details of her relationship with Massimo belonged only between the two of them. She didn't want to share them with anyone else. Not that she'd be able to do so with the man sitting right next to her, playing with her curls, trying to distract her from the conversation on purpose.

"I don't have much talent as a writer, you know."

Bree snorted in contempt. "Fess up, Charli! Is it true what they say about Italian men? That they're great in bed?"

"I have no idea." She felt herself smile, looked at Massimo. "I haven't tried them all." He raised his brows in silent question.

Bree groaned. "Okay, what about Massimo?"

"I have no way to compare; he's my first Italian." Charli gave Massimo a wicked grin and he glowered at her, while trailing his finger along her collarbone.

"You're not going to tell me a thing, are you?"

"Nope."

Massimo lowered his hand, let his fingertips dance gently over her breast, tickling her nipple. It responded instantly. The thin fabric of her bra and blouse was not much of a barrier.

"Okay, fine," Bree said, pseudo offended. "Don't tell me anything about all that hot passion you must be having. Just tell me you're having a good time."

Charli bit her lip. Massimo was exploring, his fingers working open the row of buttons on her blouse. "Yes, I'm having a very good time."

Good, Massimo mouthed in response to her last sentence. His hand worked the front clasp of her bra. In another moment she was going to be half-naked in the moonlight. Charli took in a slow breath.

"You are so lucky," Bree said with envy blooming in her voice. "Here I am, living in this crummy apartment, having a crummy job and not even a crummy man. And look at you—a sexy Italian lover, a fancy villa, months of adventure in sunny Italy.''

But it was all temporary. In a matter of weeks she'd be on a plane back home. Charli looked away from Massimo. ''Before you know it, Bree, you'll be driving to the airport to pick me up.''

''I know, I know. I'll be glad to see you again.''

Charli swallowed, pushing away thoughts of the future. This was the present—a warm summer night, Massimo, his hands touching her.

The bra clasp opened. His hand was warm as he cupped her left breast. It was becoming increasingly difficult to keep her attention on the conversation without giving away what was going on. So she did what had to be done: she said goodbye to Bree and allowed Massimo to have his Italian way with her body.

Dragging a dilapidated duffel bag, Mindy the renter arrived, droopy with fatigue and despair. Long coppery hair, sad brown eyes, like a cocker spaniel who'd lost his buddy.

She *had* lost her buddy. Her once-loving man had taken off with a dental technician.

It was soon clear that Mindy from Minnesota was focused on writing her doctoral thesis and not the type likely to invite twenty of her friends to come to Italy to drink and party, destroying Charli's lovely place in the process.

Which was the main thing. A lot of work had been done in record time, due to Massimo's influence, and it all looked bright and clean and comfortable.

''I think this will work fine,'' Mindy said after Charli had shown her around the apartment. ''It looks very nice,'' she added with a sad smile that seemed to take a lot of effort.

Charli had stocked the kitchen with food and wine as a welcome, but she soon realized she might as well have saved herself the trouble. Mindy didn't eat dairy because it gave her a skin rash. She didn't drink wine and she didn't like seafood and coffee upset her stomach. How she was going to survive on the Italian coast was a mystery to Charli, but it was not her concern. Mindy seemed nice enough, in a depressed and absent sort of way, and Charli hoped that the cheery Italian surroundings might do her good.

Which thought somehow meandered into the thought that she herself would be leaving behind cheery Italy in only a month, leaving behind Massimo. That a long lonely frozen winter loomed ahead in Philadelphia. Looking at Mindy, she almost got depressed herself.

"Well, I think that's all," she said to Mindy, and offered the brightest smile she could muster.

She got out of there fast, leaving behind good wishes, e-mail address, phone numbers, and taking with her the food Mindy didn't want to spoil because she wasn't going to eat it.

Taking a taxi, Charli rushed back to the villa, to Massimo, who was in his office. He looked so good, so warm, so alive, so sexy, so…real. How could their affair ever end?

He moved his chair away from the desk and drew her onto his knees. He stroked her cheek, lifted her chin to tilt her face up to him.

"What's wrong, *cara*?"

She swallowed hard. If only she could tell him she didn't want their affair to end when she left. That it made her sad and depressed to think of having to say goodbye to him forever. She didn't want it to be over. But she couldn't tell him that. It wasn't the plan.

"The renter, Mindy…she looked so sad, Massimo."

"Then it is good she came here. Surely she will be happy here in beautiful Italy." His voice was full of assurance. And then his mouth touched hers, his lips warm and tender, and she put her arms around him, pushing all thoughts aside, feeling only the moment and Massimo's touch, making magic with her.

"What would you like?" he whispered in her ear.

"To lock the door," she said.

"Good idea. And after that?"

"What do you have available? Do you have a menu?"

"No menu, but there's a choice of two chef's specials. We can do something slow and sweet and simmering or we can cook up something fast and hot and spicy."

"I like everything," she said, "as long as it's Italian."

"I've noticed," he said.

The day finally arrived when Valentina's cast came off. Valentina was aghast at the look of her naked leg. It had shriveled to a stick. Dead skin was peeling off in sheets. She couldn't bend her knee, she couldn't bend her ankle—both frozen into immobility because of the cast. She was in tears. It hurt to try and walk and she still relied on the crutches to move. Massimo was all tender loving care, and it warmed Charli's heart to see him tend to his sister, encouraging her patiently. Every day a physical therapist arrived to work with her and Valentina did her best, wanting to get back to school as soon as possible. Stairs remained the problem and stairs she needed to conquer.

"I'm planning a trip to South America next month," Massimo told them several days later while they were having dinner on the terrace.

Charli didn't hear all the details of their talk, some of it in Italian when they forgot she was there. After all, this was not an issue that she was involved with. Massimo would be flying out a week after she'd left Italy.

Another plan, another indication that their affair would come to an end in a matter of weeks. She did not want to think about it. Instead she wanted to look forward to going to Rome and staying with Massimo in his apartment there until she had to fly home. They'd go as soon as Valentina could go back to school. Rome would be wonderful.

Charli forked in some *gnocchi* and gave herself a mental pep talk. She was strong. She was being realistic. She knew what she was doing. It made no sense to dwell on what could not be. Soon she'd be back in Philadelphia, in her own apartment and start over. She'd just do it.

As if to affirm these thoughts, her cellphone pealed its cheery jingle and she went inside to answer it.

A call from the high school where sometimes she would substitute for a teacher who was sick or otherwise not able to work. Bree had given them her number.

One of their English teachers was going on maternity leave in January for two months. Was Charli interested in taking over her classes for that period?

Of course she was! She loved that school and the people working there. And the money would help. She'd had a lot of expenses fixing up the apartment, although most of them had been covered by the money left in the account she had also inherited. Somehow she would manage to juggle her long-distance teaching job at the same time, since the hours were hers to choose. For two months she could do it. And it would keep her busy, which would certainly be a blessing. The last thing she needed was to sit around her Philadelphia apartment in the dead of winter, nursing a broken heart.

Back at the table, she told Massimo and Valentina of

the call. Valentina stared at her with an odd look on her face.

"Did you *have* to take that job?" she asked.

"Nobody put a gun to my head, no, but I like teaching."

"You could stay here, you know. You're working on the computer all the time anyway."

Charli's heart began a nervous rhythm. "I have to be back for my parents' thirtieth wedding anniversary. It's a big deal, you know. Besides, the apartment is rented out for the next six months." She tried to sound matter-of-fact. It was a matter-of-fact business, her arrangement with Massimo. Wasn't it?

"Yes, I know," Valentina said impatiently. "But after the party you could come back and stay in Rome with Massimo. We could still see each other, go shopping together."

Charli's heart contracted as she watched Massimo's face freeze over. "Valentina," he said in a wintry tone, "Charli answered your question. This is not your business."

Charli's chest tightened. Massimo's cold expression frightened her. Where had this come from? Who was this man? Her hand trembled as she reached for her glass and took a deep swallow of wine.

Valentina stared at her plate, her face bleak. "I don't get it."

You don't get what? Charli wanted to ask, but thought better about opening her mouth and saying anything at all. Besides, she had a pretty good idea what the answer was.

Massimo too, decided no reply was necessary and ate his food.

"You are crazy about each other!" Valentina burst out.

"Charli, how can you just go away?" Her voice was full of pleading.

I'm not just going away. I have no choice.

"It's the way it has to be. Life is complicated." Her heart thumped miserably.

Valentina stared at the flowers on the table, apparently considering her next strategy. Then she lifted her face and looked at Massimo, her eyes full of challenge.

"If you'd ask her, she'd stay with you, Massimo, I know she would!"

CHAPTER TWELVE

CHARLI had done battle with herself on a few occasions lately, her less virtuous self tempted to pump Valentina for information about her brother in an effort to learn more about his marriage and what was going on in his head. Her better self had prevailed. There was something not quite honorable about taking advantage of Massimo's sister in that way.

Now, as Charli sat at the table with the two of them, Valentina's passionate plea came as a surprise and her stomach lurched in trepidation. Massimo's stony gaze met hers, then moved over to his sister.

''Valentina!'' His voice was steely as he went on speaking in Italian, saying something clearly lacking in warmth and joy.

In response to his words, Valentina stiffened, her face mutinous. ''You're being so stupid, Massimo!'' she said in English. ''Just because Giulia died! I mean, it's *ages* ago! And I didn't even like her!''

An ominous silence throbbed in the air. Even the candle flickered nervously.

''I think you've said enough,'' Massimo said with barely contained anger. ''Eat your food and go to your room.''

Valentina reached for her crutches and, without another word, hobbled away from the table, her food uneaten.

Massimo lifted the wine bottle and filled their glasses. Charli watched him, trying to read his face. There was nothing there—a mask carved out of stone, like a marble statue.

"She didn't mean to make you angry, Massimo. She just doesn't understand."

"Apparently not," he said coolly.

They finished the meal in silence and later, in bed, Massimo did not reach for her, did not touch her at all. Charli felt a terrible suspicion rise in her. He wasn't only angry about what Valentina had said.

She leaned on one elbow and looked down at his face, that beautiful face with its aristocratic nose, those dark eyes looking at her with an expression she couldn't fathom.

"Are you thinking I put her up to asking these questions?" she asked.

"Did you?"

She closed her eyes, feeling misery seep through her blood. "No, Massimo, I didn't."

"Good." He closed his eyes as if dismissing her.

His cool response suddenly made her hot with anger. She sat up, fought the onslaught of emotion.

"What the hell is wrong with you, Massimo? Why is it so terrible to talk about these things? Why do you get so angry when we mention the future, or Giulia? If she loved you, wouldn't she want you to be happy again? Why don't you want to look at the future and think of happy things? Of love, and…a wife and babies and…and…" Her voice trailed away as she saw the look in his eyes, the naked misery there, the need, the wanting.

Tears were sliding down her face. She wiped at them, but they kept on coming. "Massimo…what are you afraid of?"

But he didn't answer her. He just reached for her and kissed her silent. And she wound her arms around him, wanting to soothe the desolation she'd seen in his eyes, the misery in her own heart. How could she fight an unknown enemy?

He made love to her in a desperate hungry way that tore at her heart.

In the days that followed they did not discuss what had happened that evening, but Charli couldn't forget the look of pain and longing on his face. What kind of woman would it take to make him want to look at the future again? If she couldn't, then who could? It was not a happy thought, so she tried not to give it space.

With Valentina's walking getting better by the day, they made arrangements for the move to Rome. Charli visited Mindy at the apartment to see if everything was in order. It was. Mindy didn't look any happier, but said she'd started her work and it was going well.

Massimo's apartment in Rome was an amazing place, all comfort and luxury in a building more than four centuries old, full of interesting artwork from all over the world. Charli wandered around looking at the paintings and sculptures, asking questions, listening with fascination to Massimo's tales. Each piece had a story of how and where he had obtained it.

A party invitation for their first Saturday in Rome had her searching through her meager supply of clothes in a panic. If only she'd brought her little black and silver dress with her from Philadelphia. Richard had made her buy it for one of his company parties and it would have worked here, only it was hanging in her closet on the other side of the ocean.

She needed a new dress. And where better to find one than in Italy?

Shopping in the luxurious stores in Rome was an adventure, but the prices were a shocker. Not knowing what exactly she was looking for didn't help. She wanted something elegant but not too formal. And not *too* elegant either, actually, because she just wasn't the elegant type, was she? It would look funny on her, as if she were playing dress-up. So, where did that leave her? Not too elegant, not too formal, but festive enough for a dressy party. Or dressy enough for a festive party. Dressy, but not stuffy. Stylish. Yes, that was the word. Stylish.

Girl, she said to herself, you are making yourself crazy. By day three she could give tours to the clothing stores in Rome and still she had no dress. Clearly, something was wrong with her. Surely there was a dress somewhere in Rome for her. Rome, Italy, for heaven's sake!

Charli knew what was wrong with her: she was nervous about the damn party. Nervous she was not sophisticated enough, smart enough. What a sorry state to be in. She should be ashamed of herself.

Then in a small shop she finally found what she was looking for—a short, slinky little dress that matched her generally happy mood perfectly. It was playful and flirty in a stylish sort of way, if there was such a thing. The silky fabric felt sensuous against her skin and the sapphire color made her eyes look even bluer.

It was perfect. All her confidence came rushing back.

''What do you think?'' she asked Massimo the night of the party. She twirled around in front of him to show off the dress and make the skirt swirl sexily around her thighs.

''You look stunning, *cara*,'' he said, and the look in his eyes was confirmation enough she'd done right.

And as she stood there twirling around in front of him, she realized he had never told her what to buy, had never even told her to go shopping for a dress at all. Apparently he wasn't worried about what she would wear and what his friends would think of her, wasn't worried at all she'd make the right impression, whatever that might be. He hadn't coached her in what to talk about and what subjects to avoid. And a wonderful feeling of warmth and love filled her as she looked at him, this man who seemed to like her just the way she was, who made her feel special and beautiful and loveable.

She threw her arms around him and kissed him with all the love she felt, and then somehow the dress came off because he said he liked her naked even better than dressed.

And as she reveled in the feel of his mouth and hands making music with her body, she ignored the fear that surfaced from dark corners. *Don't love him too much*, the voice said. *Soon you will leave.*

They were late arriving at the party.

The apartment to which they were invited resembled the movie set of a historical drama—ornate antique furniture gleamed with regal elegance, crystal chandeliers glittered, exotic carpets glowed like jewels on pale marble floors. The people, however, were not in costume, but gleamed and glittered in a more contemporary fashion.

One beautiful, sophisticated woman made a special impression. An old friend, Massimo had said when he introduced her, but Charli's feminine intuition told her that the elegant Elena had ambitions beyond being an old friend. Massimo, however, paid her no special attention, and besides, if he wanted this Elena, he would have had her, wouldn't he?

Charli was happy she'd gone shopping and bought herself a new dress, because with all the elegance floating around among the antiques she would surely have felt way out of her league fashion-wise. Italian women dressed up and they did it very well. They had a way of carrying themselves that made them look elegant and gorgeous.

"Having a good time?" Massimo whispered in her ear as he entwined his fingers with hers.

"Oh, yes," she said. "This is a very interesting experience. What about you?"

"Not so interesting for me," he said and smiled at her wickedly. "I keep looking at you and my head loses all intelligent thought, which makes me useless for important conversation."

She widened her eyes in innocent shock. "You mean I make you dumb and dull?"

"No, that's not what I mean." He sighed helplessly. "I think we should go home and I will explain it to you."

Her feet hurt and Charli found a terrace in a cobblestoned side street and ordered a *caffè fredo*. A little caffeine to perk up her wilted energy. All day she'd been roaming the city and now it was time to go home. *Back to the apartment*, she corrected herself. *It is not home.* She pushed the thought away.

She sipped the glass of sweet, cold coffee and observed the other people sitting at the small tables, mostly Italians, drinking lurid yellow drinks and munching potato chips. Across the street the plastered buildings had green shutters and looked in need of a power wash. The shops on the street-level, however, were chic and upscale—all big-name Italian designers.

She loved walking around Rome, seeing all the famous sites she had known from pictures and television only, and was in awe of the beautiful architecture and art all around, so much more impressive now that she saw it all in reality. The October weather was perfection and she loved the atmosphere of the city. In the evenings they went out to dinner to wonderful restaurants, with Massimo's friends or just the two of them.

At night they slept curled up together. Waking up next to Massimo each morning filled her with bliss.

Her coffee finished, Charli paid and set off in the direction of the Piazza Venezia, looking forward to the evening with Massimo.

She felt happy. She felt happy most of the time these days.

It's all a dream, she told herself one morning as she looked down on Massimo's sleeping face. *One day soon you will wake up and it will be over. He will no longer sleep next to you.* The thought filled her with sudden terror. *Stop it, stop it*, she admonished herself. *Enjoy what you have now*.

And what was it that she had now?

A temporary love affair with a handsome, charming Italian.

And she'd made the fatal mistake of falling in love.

No, it was more than that. It was more than just that passionate, hot, tremulous feeling of floating and being in love. The feeling had grown roots, was deeper, less transient. Love. She loved him. He had become part of her, had wriggled his way into her heart with his warm smile, his affectionate touching and the way he looked at her as if she was the most precious thing on earth. He liked her just the way she was. He was loving and considerate and funny and sometimes a tad too arrogant, too authoritarian, but it was part of his Italian nature and she loved him.

Oh, God, she thought, how can I give him up now?

If only she could tell him she loved him, that she wanted him always. That she wanted to be married and have babies and celebrate a thirty-year wedding anniversary.

But she couldn't tell him that. She'd made a deal, an unspoken agreement, and she should keep to it. Besides, she had her pride. She wasn't going to beg for something he wouldn't offer freely.

But there was always the secret hope whispering at the edges of her consciousness. Could Massimo change his mind? Would he really want to end what they had together?

He never mentioned it, never talked about her leaving, as if it was not something he ever even thought about.

If it ended as he wanted it to, if he let her leave and didn't ask her to come back to him, would she be able to bear it?

She would have to. She'd have to start over. Start another chapter in her life.

Wrapped in her kimono, Charli stood in front of her dressing table and searched for a pair of earrings she wanted to wear. She watched Massimo in the mirror. He took off his jacket and tie and pulled his shirt out of his trousers. She liked watching him take off his clothes, even if only because he wanted to change before they were going out to dinner. She liked seeing his lean brown hands work the buttons on his shirt. He shrugged out of it, exposing his chest and flat brown stomach. She loved the way the soft, dark chest hair tapered down and disappeared below his belt.

His movements were all familiar. She knew what was coming next. He'd sit down on the side of the bed and pull off his shoes and socks, then get up again and unbuckle his belt, slide down the zip and take off his trousers.

Ten days left. After that she'd be home again, alone,

and watching the simple ritual of Massimo's undressing would be something of the past.

She was making herself miserable counting down the days to her departure, but she couldn't help herself.

Hope kept peeking around the corner of her thoughts. Maybe Massimo would change his mind about ending the affair. Because he loved her. Because he could not bear to think of his life without her in it.

When it's over, it's over.

Hope was a terrible traitor.

She kept wondering about his wife, what hold she had on him even now after all those years. But she knew better than to broach that subject again.

She found the earrings and put them aside. She'd have a quick shower before dressing for dinner. In the mirror she saw Massimo sit down on the edge of the bed—her side of the bed—and on the bedside table her cellphone rang.

He picked it up and handed it to her. She flipped it open and found the high school in Philadelphia on the line. She listened with growing trepidation as someone explained to her that the teacher she was going to take over for in January had problems with her pregnancy and on doctor's orders had to stop working and stay home.

Was it possible for Charli to take over immediately? How long would it take her to get back to Philadelphia?

Not much time at all.

Her little apartment was already dealt with. Her clothes were here in Rome. Flights to the States left every day.

Ten days until she'd been planning to leave. Ten days with Massimo. It was all she had left. Her departure date felt like doomsday in her mind, looming ever closer. Depression was settling in already, casting a shadow over the joy of being with Massimo.

She glanced over at him, standing there naked but for his black Italian briefs, looking sinfully sexy with his hair rumpled and his eyes full of deep secrets she would never know. Her Italian lover.

That was what he was and all he would ever be. There was no hope for the future. The torture of that knowledge was getting to her. She couldn't take it anymore.

When it's over, it's over.

So why not just be done with it and start her life over now instead of stretching out the agony for another ten hopeless days of longing and despair?

"I'll come as soon as I can," she heard herself say. "I'll check the flights and call you later."

Her hand trembled as she put the phone down. She felt as if she'd just jumped from a plane without a parachute. Massimo was pulling on another pair of trousers and looked at her with his eyebrows raised.

"What's wrong?" he asked, his tone alarmed. "Are you leaving?"

She looked at him, the man who liked her just the way she was, who made such wonderful love to her, who made her feel beautiful and desirable. Oh, God, she thought, what have I done? Surely they could have found someone else? What possessed me to agree? I can't leave him.

You have to leave him, said a little voice.

She swallowed. Her throat ached. She couldn't talk.

"Charli!" He sat down next to her on the side of the bed and took her hand.

She took a deep breath, swallowed again, gathered as much composure and pride as she could and manufactured a little smile.

"Yes, I have to leave earlier than I thought. Tomorrow, probably."

"What?" His voice exploded into the air. "You can't

leave just yet!'' Dark eyes flashing, hands gesturing, he was the very image of an outraged Latin lover. "I want you here, in my arms, in my bed!"

For another ten days, and then he'd let her go. After all, that was the plan and he had given no indication he wanted to change it.

"I'm sorry," she said, trying desperately to keep her emotions under control. She needed to be businesslike about this.

"Why?" His eyes were full of smoldering fire. "Why do you have to go?"

So she told him about the problem, and her decision.

He was quiet for a moment, his body tense and still.

"Are you telling me they couldn't find someone else and they're dragging you all the way back from Italy?"

"They may well be able to find someone else. The trouble is they don't want the kids to have to deal with a change of teacher more often than necessary. It doesn't promote learning."

"What if you had said no?"

"I might lose the job in January if the person they find can stay for the whole period that the teacher is gone."

She couldn't afford to lose that job, and it was more than money she needed. She'd need to be busy.

"It's only a matter of nine days if I leave tomorrow, Massimo," she said as if nine days was nothing. Nine days of being together, eating together, making love together.

She came to her feet and headed for the bathroom, wanting nothing more than to escape.

All it would take for her to stay was for him to ask her to be part of his life, his future. Surely he understood that?

"Very well, then," he said behind her, his voice controlled now and businesslike. "I am not happy to see you leave so soon, but this is your decision."

She caught his bleak expression in the mirror and her heart contracted. She went into the bathroom, turned on the shower and got in. But all the water pouring over her didn't help calm her and she found herself crying silently, miserably.

As planned, they went out to dinner at the Boccondivino with some of Massimo's friends. She managed to live through it, although she hardly tasted the food, which was a crime since it was reputed to be superb. Massimo seemed in fine shape, laughing and having a good time. She hated him for it.

Feeling helpless, angry and desperate all at the same time, she wished all of this was over. One painful lesson she had learned from this Italian adventure: she simply was not the type to have a temporary love affair and walk away untouched afterward. She was touched in every possible way.

Unexpectedly, the elegant Elena joined them halfway through, which didn't do Charli's mood any good. The woman was a huntress and her eyes were on her prey.

Charli kept watching Massimo and wondered time and again what made him so afraid of the future. She drank more wine than she should have, forcing herself to be cheery.

"You are leaving next week, yes?" Elena asked. Her tone was casual enough, but Charli suspected the woman couldn't wait to see her gone. Well, she had good news for her.

"Actually, no," she said, smiling, sipping more wine. "I'm catching a flight tomorrow."

"Oh, really?" Elena's eyes widened, then she smiled.

"Well, then…" She turned to Massimo, rattled off something in Italian Charli couldn't begin to grasp.

Well, for all she cared the woman might have invited herself into his bed. It was none of her business what happened after tomorrow. She finished her wine and a waiter duly poured her some more.

Back at the apartment later, Massimo got ready for bed while she lingered until he came up to her, put his arms around her and, without a word, began to kiss her passionately while nudging her toward the bed, lowering her onto it.

"This is our last night. Let's not waste it, *cara*," he whispered. "I will miss you."

She wanted to lash out at him in anger, say hurtful things, make him hurt like she was hurting herself, yet all she did was kiss him back with a desperate hunger.

One last night.

She clung to him all through the endless dark hours and as she lay awake she silently begged him to say the words she wanted to hear.

He didn't say them.

When morning came she made herself freeze over, forced herself not to feel. Like an automaton she went through the motions of showering and dressing and getting her suitcases closed.

She called a taxi to take her to the airport, which displeased Massimo when she told him.

"Don't be foolish. I shall drive you, of course," he said in an authoritarian tone that severely annoyed her.

She glared at him. Her anger was her friend. It protected her from going to pieces. "Don't order me around, Massimo! I *want* to take a taxi." She was going to Valentina's school first to say goodbye, then on to the airport. Dragging out her goodbye to Massimo would only make things worse. "Just go to your office and work. I'll be fine."

He scowled at her, his chin steely. "It's all right for you to order me around?"

She shrugged. "I'll be gone in ten minutes, so who cares?" She turned around as her eyes filled with tears. She couldn't stand it. This was the end, and they were sniping at each other. She felt as if she was about to fall apart.

He wrapped his arms around her, turning her around, then put her head against his chest. He smelled familiar, felt familiar. He was everything she loved and wanted. She felt him stroking her hair.

"This is no way to say goodbye," he said softly. "We must not part in anger. You are a very special woman, Charli, and I will always treasure…"

She pushed herself away. "Oh, shut *up*, Massimo! I *so* don't want to hear this now!" Her body rigid, she fought the urge to cry and stamp her feet and tell him he was a coward and a—

Stop it! stop it! she admonished herself. *Have a little class.*

Where the strength came from, she would never know. But as the bell rang to announce the arrival of the taxi, she squared her shoulders, tugged down her shirt and looked right at him.

"Okay, you're right, this isn't any way to part." She stood on tiptoe, kissed him quickly on the mouth and smiled. "Goodbye, Massimo. Thank you for a wonderful time in Italy."

CHAPTER THIRTEEN

"WHAT do you want to do tonight?" Bree asked.

Charli shifted the phone to her other hand and looked out the window. It was snowing again. The winter had started early and was dragging on. It was only the first week in January and much more nasty weather was to come for certain. She felt like crawling under the covers and not coming out until spring. She wanted to close her eyes on the misery in her heart and not wake up until she could feel the sun again.

That not being a possibility, she'd better figure out what to do with this Saturday night.

"What are the options?" she asked.

"We can dress up and see if we can find some action at the Shangri-La."

"No."

"I can call my new neighbors across the hall and see if they want to go out to dinner to that new Ethiopian restaurant."

"No."

"We can rent some psycho-thrillers, get a bottle of wine, order Chinese and stay in."

"Perfect."

She wouldn't have to dress up or be charming to those new people. She just wanted to stay home. She didn't even feel like expending the energy to go over to Bree's place on the next block. "Come over here," she said. "I have wine and a box of really good chocolates. And if you're too scared to go home alone later, you can just crash on the couch.''

Later, as she cleared the coffee table of books and papers to make space for the food and the wine, she wondered if she was being fair to Bree. She was a bore. She didn't want to go out, didn't feel like dating. Couldn't bear the thought of another man touching her, kissing her.

Before putting away the laptop, she checked her e-mail and found a message from Valentina. *Charli*, she wrote, *the Caribbean is awesome!*

She and Massimo were spending the winter holidays with family members in sunny Martinique and apparently this was a success, apart from the fact that Elena was there also and Valentina didn't like her. *She treats me like I'm ten years old!* Valentina wrote.

Charli stopped reading, tried to breathe. Something was wrong with her to feel such pain at the thought of that woman with Massimo. Was Elena the next one in a line of temporary affairs?

Elena was an old friend, Massimo had said when he'd introduced them, and he'd never lied to her or deceived her as far as she knew. But what was true then was not necessarily true today. Massimo had every right to have an affair with anyone he pleased.

Charli swallowed at the constriction in her throat. She was an idiot to keep feeling so devastated every time she thought of Massimo. But she had no control over her feelings—they were there and they refused to go.

She took an unsteady breath and tried to focus on Valentina's message on the screen.

Now and again, Valentina sent her a message, usually nothing more than a few hastily typed lines, but Charli was always happy to hear from her. She had fully expected Valentina to be too busy with her school life to ever give much thought to her, Charli, now that she was no longer a presence in her daily life.

She closed the laptop and put it away.

Bree arrived, bringing in a wave of cold air and a happy grin. "I just love all this snow! You wanna go outside and play? Make a snowman?"

"No, I want to be in the Caribbean, in the sun." It slipped out before she could think about it.

Bree laughed as she dumped her bag by the door and flipped back the hood of her coat. Her long red hair tumbled around her rosy-cold face. She unzipped her coat. "Well, that's progress. Up to now you just wanted to be in Italy."

"I just got an e-mail from Valentina. They're in Martinique for the holidays." She left out the news that Elena was there also. She didn't feel like analyzing her feelings. Her useless, irrelevant feelings.

Bree shouldered out of her coat and frowned. "So no progress."

"I'm a big bore, I'm sorry. I just never knew I could miss somebody that much."

Never had she known such utter desolation. She'd tried to hate him for hurting her, but she was incapable of it. He was the man she wanted, the man she loved.

Never again, she thought. Never again will I fall in love and let myself in for this kind of agony. I can't stand it. I just can't stand it.

Bree was looking at her, concern in her eyes. "Charli," she said slowly, "I'm beginning to think you should do something."

"Do something? Like what? Jump off a bridge?"

"Like tell him you love him."

Charli stared at Bree, digesting the words. She thought of the terrible day she had left Rome, of Massimo letting her go. She thought of Elena. She gave a bitter little laugh. "You've got to be kidding."

"It's the truth, Charli, and he doesn't know it."

"He should know it! He *has* to know it!"

"But you never *told* him!"

"And you think that might have changed his mind about wanting a future with a wife and kids in it?"

Bree sighed with exasperation. "I don't know, Charli, and neither do you. But if he is the man you want, maybe you should fight for him."

Charli said nothing. She felt utterly helpless. How did you fight for a man who didn't want you?

Bree hung up her coat and picked up her bag. "Enough said." She plopped herself down on the sofa and fished out a couple of video cassettes. "Let's watch a movie."

Several weeks later the weather had not improved, but at least her teaching job kept her mind busy most of the time if not all of the time. In unguarded moments she kept thinking of what Bree had said, and always the question returned in her head: how did you fight for a man who didn't want you? If he wanted her, Massimo knew exactly where to find her.

And a few weeks later he did.

Seeing his name and address in the In Box of her e-mail program came as a shock. Her heart crashed against her ribs, then started pounding like mad. She opened the message.

Dear Charli,
I trust you are well. I am writing concerning Valentina. You've probably already been informed by her that I have finally relented. She will start her studies at the University of Pennsylvania in September.

I will have business in New York at the end of February and would like to come to Philadelphia to see you and discuss my concerns about Valentina being so far away from home. May I take you out to dinner?

Regards, Massimo.

He was coming to Philadelphia and he wanted to see her. About Valentina. Of course Charli knew about his change of heart, had received a jubilant couple of lines from Valentina not long ago.

She read the message again. It was a very businesslike little note which could have been directed to anyone. Nothing personal to indicate they had once shared some very un-businesslike nights and days.

He wanted to meet with her. Talk about Valentina.

Damn him! she thought suddenly, as a painful rage surged through her. *He doesn't want me in his life, but he wants me in Valentina's. I'm not going to let him do this to me. I don't want to see him. I couldn't bear it.*

Her head hurt. The headache she'd been nursing all day was turning ugly.

The thought of seeing him again, sitting across from him and having a polite conversation about Valentina filled her with dread. How could she possibly manage not to fall apart?

Because she was a strong person, that was why. She had her pride. She had her dignity. She had her cussed American toughness.

She replied to his message in an equally businesslike tone, telling him to let her know when he was in town and she'd meet with him.

She hit *Send* and got up, her head pounding. She felt like death.

*   *   *

It wasn't just a headache but a case of full-blown flu and she spent the next week in bed, feverish and semi-delirious, dreaming twisted dreams of Massimo, which fortunately she lost as soon as she awoke. In her more conscious episodes, she wished for oblivion while she coughed herself dizzy. With her parents in Hawaii on a winter vacation, Bree took care of her like the good friend she was.

It took another week to get back to something resembling normal.

One cold and frigid Saturday morning she was gripped by the urge to cook. This hadn't happened once in the last few months, so it was nothing short of a miracle, and possibly a sign of something, but she didn't know what. She went shopping and then took her time putting together an old-fashioned beef stew with fresh ingredients, actually taking pleasure in the activity of cutting carrots and onions and potatoes, cleaning plump mushrooms, browning the onions and chunks of meat. She washed a bunch of parsley and set it in a glass on the counter, enjoying the rich, lush green of the pretty leaves. After the misery of the flu it was good to feel alive again.

She went back to work grading English papers while the stew bubbled away on the stove, filling the apartment with its lovely homey aroma. This was not gourmet cooking, but it was good for the soul on a winter night.

By six the stew was ready. She adjusted the seasoning and added a glass of red wine for a decadent touch, although that wasn't part of the recipe. She tasted the final result. It was very, very delicious.

She was reaching for a big bowl when the phone rang.

"Hello?" she said into the mouthpiece.

"Charli?"

Her heart stopped. Then started racing. She knew that voice, would recognize it anywhere, anytime.

"Hello, Massimo."

He was at the airport, he told her, and apologized for not ringing her earlier but his plans had changed. Could she meet with him tomorrow for lunch, or was it at all possible for him to come over now and take her to dinner this evening?

Her mind scrambled feverishly considering the positives and negatives of the two choices, the worst negative of the lunch plan being that she'd be awake all night going crazy waiting for tomorrow. She just wanted it over with.

"Just come over now," she said.

She looked a mess. She'd been cooking wearing an old sweatshirt and ancient jeans. No make-up graced her pale winter face and she looked sixteen. Her hair needed a shampoo. No way did she want him to see her like this.

She rushed into the bedroom, stripped off her clothes, dashed into the shower. Thank God it would take him a while to get here from the airport.

When the doorbell rang she was ready, wearing clean jeans and a soft fuchsia sweater, casual but nice. Her face was made-up and her hair was washed and dry—well, just about. The color of the wool sweater was cheery. She wanted to look cheery. And happy. And perfectly fine. She wanted to look as if she had been doing just brilliantly without him in her life.

She buzzed open the downstairs front door. It would take him a couple of minutes to climb the three flights of stairs and she stood by her apartment door, waiting for him, her heart pounding wildly. No matter what she said to herself, she couldn't feel calm.

The man standing in front of her was a stranger. He

didn't look like she remembered him. Wearing a long wool overcoat, a scarf and leather gloves, he looked quite imposing and elegant and totally alien. His right hand gripped the handle of a small overnight carry-bag on wheels. She assumed he'd made a hotel reservation somewhere.

"Hello, Massimo," she said politely. She moved aside to let him in and closed the door behind him.

He put the bag down and smiled at her.

"Hello, Charli." He took both her hands in his gloved ones, leaned forward and kissed her on both cheeks—right, left, right. *"Come sta?"* He looked right into her eyes.

All strangeness fled. He was the Massimo she knew, all right. The same warm brown eyes looking straight into hers, the same charm.

"I'm fine," she lied. She wondered if he could hear the sound of her heart pounding.

He released her hands. "You look beautiful, as I remember," he said, taking off his gloves.

"Thank you," she said politely. His Italian charm in her American living room seemed a bit out of place.

"I apologize if I inconvenience you by coming with so little notice."

"It's not a problem."

He glanced at his watch. "It is not too early for dinner in America, so perhaps you know a suitable restaurant nearby?"

"We can stay here. I have food." She didn't know why she invited him, except that it came to her naturally. She would have said that to anyone coming here tonight. It was freezing cold outside, and she had a pan of stew on the stove.

"You are so generous, but no, I cannot accept. I promised you—"

"Massimo, it's freezing out there. I'd rather not go out and I can give you a superb American dining experience right here in my humble abode."

"Abode?"

She made a grand sweeping gesture. "My residence," she said loftily. "The place where I live."

He glanced around. "It's very nice, warm—it shows your personality."

"Thank you. It's a bit small, but I like it." Such a polite little conversation, she thought dryly, and under the surface I'm a nervous wreck. She ran her fingers through her curls. Underneath they still felt slightly damp.

His attention had been caught by a painting on her wall, done by an artist friend.

"Take off your coat," she said, "please. You can hang it over there." She pointed at the rack by the door.

He hesitated, then without further comment he shrugged out of the coat. He wore a dark business suit, a gorgeous silk tie and a white shirt. His hair, stylishly long, touched the collar of his shirt. Thick, dark and silky, it begged to be touched and for an agonizing moment she remembered the feel of it against her hands, her skin.

Don't go there, she admonished herself. *Be cool. You can do this.*

You have to do this.

He pushed his jacket back and slipped his hands in his trouser pockets. "So what is this superb American dining experience you are offering me?" His voice, warm and deep, curled through her like dark honey.

"A one-pot meal. No *antipasto*, no *primo*, no *secondo*, no *contorni*. Maybe dessert, we'll see." Did she have ice cream in the freezer?

He arched his left eyebrow in amusement. "And what is the name of this food?"

"Stew. Beef stew, to be exact. Surely you've had something like it in England when you studied there."

"Yes, I have, I remember. Everything cooked together in sauce." The tone of his voice did not speak of much admiration.

She almost laughed, amazing herself. "Yes. And the way I make it is very good. And we might as well have some right now if you're hungry. Oh, and I have wine. A California syrah, very American, very good also. Would you mind opening the bottle?"

"Not at all. Where can I wash my hands?"

"Oh, sorry, over there." She pointed at the bathroom door. "Clean towels on the rack on the wall."

She'd wanted to be cold and businesslike, but she couldn't manage it. It was not in her to be cold and businesslike with this man. She'd wanted to hate him for not loving her enough, and she couldn't do that either. A terrible despair rose inside her and she cursed herself for her stupidity. Cold or not cold, she should have gone out to a restaurant with him. Wouldn't it have been much easier to be calm and businesslike while eating in public than in the intimate surroundings of her own apartment?

She put her computer on the floor, out of the way, arranged place mats, napkins and bowls and glasses on the small table. Should she light the candle? It was on the table already—she always had one on the table. This was ridiculous—why was she asking herself if she should light it? She always lighted a candle when people came over for dinner.

She struck a match and held it to the wick. It flared instantly in a dance of light.

When Massimo appeared at her side she gave him the wine bottle and the opener.

"So where have you been on your travels lately?" she asked casually. She wanted to say something, talk about neutral things. "Was your trip to South America a success?"

She ladled the stew into big pottery bowls as he talked. Snipped parsley on top. Cut a loaf of crusty bread. Put some butter on the table. Kept her hands busy as she asked a question here and there, trying to concentrate on his words. The sound of his voice, rich and deep, stirred the embers of buried emotions, warming her when all she wanted was to stay cool and calm. It was so awful to still feel the same attraction, now worse because of its hopelessness.

They sat down, and she spread the napkin on her lap. She picked up her glass of wine and managed a smile at him. "A toast to Valentina's happiness," she said, and he smiled back and touched his glass gently with hers.

"To Valentina's happiness," he repeated.

They drank the wine. "Very good," he said, a sudden gleam in his eyes. "For not being Italian."

"Gee, thanks. I'll take that as a compliment. And what about the stew?"

He glanced down at the bowl in front of him. "It is superb," he said, picking up his spoon. "Because you prepared it."

What else had she expected him to say? He'd eat it no matter how bad it was, which of course it wasn't. It was superb, indeed. Which he acknowledged as they continued eating, talking about Valentina.

Halfway through the meal, the phone rang. She came to her feet and picked it up from the coffee table.

An old quavery voice asked to speak to Jake.

''There's no Jake here,'' Charli said gently, visualizing a frail old woman on the other end of the line. ''I think you have the wrong number.''

''Oh, dear. It's my glasses, they're broken. I'm sorry to bother you, honey.''

''That's all right, no problem.''

She put the phone down. Massimo was looking at her.

''Jake? Not the new man in your life?''

''No. Wrong number.'' She sat down again and picked up her napkin. ''There's no man in my life.'' She hesitated. ''What about you? Valentina wrote Elena spent the holidays with you.''

Annoyance flashed across his face. ''Elena is an old friend. A family friend, actually. That's why she was there.''

He had never lied to her. She felt a ridiculous relief, a flare of hope.

''She doesn't want to be an old friend,'' she said. ''It seemed rather obvious to me when I was in Rome.''

''Fortunately she's found more agreeable prey,'' he said dryly. ''She's hooked herself a Brazilian banana baron, so I heard last week.'' He spooned in another bite of stew, clearly not finding the subject of interest.

They continued talking about Valentina. He was concerned about her being so far away from home and not knowing anyone but her friend Melissa, whose diplomat parents were moving on to Thailand for their next post.

''I will be here,'' Charli said. ''You know I'll do anything for her.''

''I know,'' he said, and she saw the gratitude in his eyes, felt her heart fill with some warm, sad emotion she didn't have a name for. She took a swallow of wine.

''And my parents are here, and my best friend is here. We'll all be happy to help her, invite her for weekends or holidays, take care of her if there ever is a problem or a need.'' She pushed her empty bowl aside and leaned her arms on the table. ''But you know what will happen?''

He frowned. ''What?''

''She'll be so busy making her own friends, she'll not need us much. She's a big girl, Massimo, and she's smart. She's a lovely, charming girl with a good set of brains and she'll be fine here in America.''

''I'm pleased you have such confidence in her.''

She smiled. ''I got to know her pretty well in all those weeks we spent together.''

''Yes.'' He looked at her, his eyes filled with some dark emotion she could not identify, some struggle she didn't understand. He folded his napkin and put it next to his plate, saying nothing more.

''I'll make coffee,'' she said.

''No, wait.'' He reached across the table and took her hand. ''There's something I want to explain to you. We'll have coffee later.''

She swallowed. ''Sure, if you like.'' His hand was warm on hers. It felt good to be touched by him and she stared at the lean brown fingers she knew so well, fingers that knew how to make magic with her body. It was not a memory she wanted right now.

He let go of her hand and reached for the wine bottle. ''Let's finish this and sit on the sofa.''

He poured the last of the wine and they picked up their glasses and moved to the couch.

''What do you want to explain to me?'' she asked, cradling the wineglass in both her hands.

He hesitated. ''You just said you got to know Valentina well when you lived at the villa with us.'' He looked right into her eyes. ''But you didn't get to know me very well, did you?''

She felt a nervous fluttering in her chest. "Not as much as I wanted to."

"You asked me once why I didn't want to think about the future, and I never answered you."

"Right."

"I've always felt guilty for not telling you about…" He frowned, clearly having trouble expressing himself. "Do you remember the time I came to see your apartment after your kitchen was done up?"

She nodded.

"Remember you asked me why I didn't want to talk about my wife?"

She swallowed. The memory sprang up, vivid, alive. The anger in his face, his eyes, his voice. So much anger. And she remembered the night before she had left, when again she'd asked him why he didn't want to talk about the future. "Yes, I remember."

"I want to tell you about it now. I want you to understand why I let you go."

She stared down into her glass, at the ruby-red wine, and felt an unexpected heat rush to the surface. He wanted her to understand why he let her go.

How generous of him! He wanted to tell her *now*? What difference did it make if she understood now?

"You don't have to tell me anything, Massimo." Her chest felt tight and it was difficult to breathe. She looked up to meet his dark gaze, intent on her face. "It doesn't matter anymore. When it's over, it's over. That's the understanding we had."

Even if it went wrong for me in the end, she added silently.

He pushed himself to his feet, ran both hands through his hair. "Please, Charli, listen to me."

He paced. Ripped off his tie. Raked his fingers through

his hair again. Like a tiger in a cage. A tiger who wanted out.

"What I said was true," he said. "I loved her." He rubbed his face. "I thought she loved me."

A stab of surprise. Her heart skipped a beat. She said nothing.

"She died in a car accident in Firenze—Florence, I mean. I'm sure Valentina told you that much, although I'm quite sure she doesn't know the rest of the story." He closed his eyes for a moment. "Giulia had told me she was spending a week with her sister in Emilia, but I found out she'd never been there. She'd been in Firenze all along with her lover. He was driving the car. It was all over the papers and I had not the faintest notion what had been going on behind my back. She'd been with this man for over a year and I didn't know." Dark desolation in his eyes.

Out came all the pain and grief of his betrayal, of a marriage that had been a sham, of a woman who had not loved him.

"It was all a lie. An illusion."

Charli's anger had melted away. "I didn't know," she whispered, her heart aching for him. She was filled with regret for not understanding, for thinking she'd been competing with the memory of a loving wife.

He shrugged helplessly. "So, where does that leave me now? You asked me another question. *Why are you so angry?* Well, it came back to me and I kept asking myself, yes, why was I still so angry after all that time?"

He massaged his neck, as if rubbing away stress and tension. "In the beginning I was emotionally devastated because I had lost my wife. Then I became angry be-cause…because my marriage was a lie." He waved his hands. "My wife had been unfaithful to me and the woman I mourned had never even existed. I was mourning an illusion. Even my grief was meaningless. I blamed her for everything, for my unhappiness, for my distrust.''

His mouth curved down in a bittersweet smile. ''You know what? I realized not long ago that I wasn't angry with her anymore. I was angry with myself because I hadn't seen what there was to see—I was so blind about her and about our relationship, and I had failed myself.''

He fell silent and Charli said nothing. She had no great wisdom to share. She'd been so blind about her own relationship, about the kind of man Richard really was. She had also failed herself by ignoring the signals and suppressing her instincts.

He sat down next to her. Elbows on his knees, he rested his head in his hands.

''I don't trust my own instincts anymore,'' he said, his voice muffled by his hands, yet she heard the despair in his tone.

She felt an upwelling of compassion, of understanding. Tears burned behind her eyes.

If he is the man you want, maybe you should fight for him, came Bree's voice.

He looked up. ''I think I've not always been easy on Valentina, not trusting my own instincts, either. I wanted to make sure she grew up with decent values. She's beautiful and sometimes I worried that…that she might become like Giulia, breaking some fool of a guy's heart.''

''Oh, Massimo. There's more chance the other way around.''

His smile held a touch of self-derision. ''Naturally, I'm concerned about that as well.''

''Naturally,'' she said dryly. ''But you allowed her to come here to go to college, so you've decided it's time to let her try out being independent now, so you're doing all right."

He looked away for a moment, as if remembering something. "I suppose part of my problem is that I can't give up the feeling that she needs me. Like when she was little. When my parents died." He paused, staring blindly ahead. "But she's no longer ten and she doesn't really need me anymore." He sounded so bleak, Charli felt her heart contract.

"That's not true, Massimo. Of course she needs you. Just not in the way she used to. She needs to know you are there, that you are her family, that whatever happens she can turn to you because you will always love her and you will always be her big brother." She swallowed at the lump in her throat. She stood up. "I'll make coffee."

She went to the kitchen, feeling the need to get away, feeling the words she had spoken taking on a life of their own, wanting those words for herself…*you will always love me and you will always be the man in my life.*

She rinsed the coffee pot, her vision suddenly blurred by tears.

She had never planned to fall in love with him, had never wanted this, but her heart had a mind of its own.

Tears ran down her face and she wiped at them, terrified he'd notice. She was facing away from him, but across the breakfast bar he could see her back. She put fresh water in the coffee maker. Wiped at her tears again. She took out a filter and inserted it, took the coffee can and scooped coffee into the filter.

Her throat ached with the effort not to cry. She took in a slow, deep breath, trying to stay calm. She slipped the pot under the filter and flipped the switch.

She heard him get up, heard him come around the breakfast bar. The coffee maker gurgled in the silence.

He stood behind her. Head bent, she blinked furiously, her heart beating fast. She stared into the sink, afraid to look at him, her body tense all over.

"Charli?"

She still didn't look at him. "What?" Her voice sounded thick with tears. There was nothing she could do about it.

She felt his hands on her upper arms, felt him turn her around. She kept her head down but he put his hand under her chin and lifted her face. All she saw was the blur of his face.

"Charli," he said softly, "you're crying."

The tone of his voice broke something inside her. She didn't care about her pride anymore, about being strong and independent and brave. None of it mattered more than the terrible ache of loss and need inside her heart, the part that longed for him, for his arms around her, the soft whispers of his voice in her ear.

If he is the man you want, maybe you should fight for him.

"Charli, what's wrong?"

"I miss you so," she whispered.

For a fraction of a second after she heard herself say the words, Charli felt a flash of naked terror. What if he did not want to hear this?

He *had* to hear this.

With a low moan he wrapped his arms around her and pressed her close. "I missed you too," he said, his voice rough with emotion.

His words were like a balm to her raw nerves, and tears of relief flooded her eyes. A sob escaped her and he stroked her hair, murmuring words she didn't understand. Then he withdrew a little and looked at her, but all she saw was a blur.

"Charli, letting you go was the stupidest mistake I ever made. I'm so sorry I caused you pain."

She needed a tissue, couldn't remember where there was a box. She reached for the paper towels instead and mopped up her face. She drew in a shuddering breath, tried to calm down.

"But it was what we agreed," she said, her voice thick and unsteady. "When it's over, it's over." His face was in focus again and she could see the emotion smoldering in his eyes.

"But it wasn't over, *cara*."

"I thought it was, for you."

"I tried to tell myself it was. I don't know what insanity possessed me, but I was doing the same thing I had done before."

"I don't know what you mean," she said.

"I did it again. I was blind about our relationship as well. I was so frightened to ever love again and be cheated and humiliated again, that I did not see what was right in front of me. Here was true happiness staring me in the face and I did not see it." He kissed her very tenderly. "I didn't see it until after you had gone, and even then I tried to deny it for a long time."

He looked into her eyes and she saw the truth. Her heart stumbled. "You didn't come here to talk about Valentina, did you?" He could have asked her to look out for Valentina in an e-mail, or on the phone.

"No. I came to see you. To see if there was any hope left, if you still wanted me." He closed his eyes briefly. "Charli, you are the real deal, and I know that does not sound at all like a romantic Italian lover speaking, but in English this is the only way I know how to express this. The real deal. You are the true love of my heart. I love you, I adore you."

He kissed her, and her heart went soaring, and she kissed him back, and a thousand lights went on in her soul chasing the darkness and the emptiness.

She drew back and smiled up into his eyes. "You love me? Really?"

"Yes, really. *Ti amo, ti voglio bene*. I love you, I want you. I can see clearly now."

"Oh, Massimo." Tears threatened again. "I love you, too. I didn't know I could love anyone so much. I was so miserable thinking you didn't want me. That all I was to you was a temporary fling."

He groaned. "Don't say that. You were never a *fling*. What we had was real and good—I was just too stupid to see it." He took her face in his hands and looked deep into her eyes. "I'm never, never letting you go again," he whispered. *"Mai!"* he added with fervor, as if saying it in Italian made it more so.

"I'll never leave you, Massimo." She swallowed at the constriction in her throat.

"Is that a promise?" His voice sounded husky.

"Yes."

"So you will marry me?"

She smiled. "Yes. If you want me to be your wife."

A fiery love darkened his eyes. "I want you to be my wife. I want to be your husband. I want to have babies and be happy ever after."

She smiled as tears welled in her eyes. "Me too."

He kissed her again, as if he could not get enough of her, expressing with his mouth the love in his heart.

She clung to him, pressing herself into him, feeling the heat of his body. She smelled his clean, familiar scent, smelled Italy and the flavors of love, felt the sunshine and the warmth. Her body bloomed, her blood sang to his kisses and the caressing of his hands.

And then he said more to her in Italian, beautiful words and phrases not in the guidebooks.

"Non capisco," she whispered.

"Show me your bedroom," he whispered back, "and I'll explain it to you."

MILLS & BOON®

Volume 11
on sale from
7th May
2005

Lynne
GRAHAM

International Playboys

*A Vengeful
Passion*

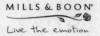

MILLS & BOON®
Live the emotion

Modern
romance™

AT THE SPANISH DUKE'S COMMAND
by Fiona Hood-Stewart

Georgiana fell for Juan Felipe Mansanto, Duque de Caniza,
even though he was supposed to be her guardian. And it
seemed that, try as he might, Juan couldn't resist her.
But Juan was about to make a marriage of convenience to
another woman…

THE SHEIKH'S VIRGIN *by Jane Porter*

Lots of women have enjoyed the benefits of being Sheikh
Kalen Nuri's mistress – but they have all bored him. Now
Kalen has discovered beautiful Keira – but she's refusing to
be his, even though she has been chosen as his virgin bride!

THE ITALIAN DOCTOR'S MISTRESS *by Catherine Spencer*

Successful neurosurgeon Carlo Rossi has a passion for his
work – and for women. And he desires Danielle Blake like
no other woman. He insists they play by his rules – no
future, just a brief affair. But when it's time for Danielle to
leave Italy can he let her go?

PREGNANT BY THE GREEK TYCOON *by Kim Lawrence*

After a passionate whirlwind marriage to Greek billionaire
Angolos Constantine, Georgie is pregnant. She is sure
Angolos will be delighted – but instead he tells her to go
away and never come back…but he'll have what's his – by
whatever means necessary.

Don't miss out…

On sale 6th May 2005

*Available at most branches of WHSmith, Tesco, ASDA, Martins,
Borders, Eason, Sainsbury's and all good paperback bookshops.*

Visit www.millsandboon.co.uk

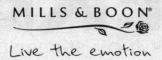

MILLS & BOON®

Live the emotion

Her Greek Millionaire

Have these gorgeous Greek multimillionaires met their match?

In May 2005, By Request brings back three favourite romances by our bestselling Mills & Boon authors:

The Husband Test *by Helen Bianchin*
The Kyriakis Baby *by Sara Wood*
The Greek Tycoon's Bride
by Helen Brooks

Make sure you get hold of these passionate stories, on sale 6th May 2005

4 FREE

BOOKS AND A SURPRISE GIFT!

We would like to take this opportunity to thank you for reading this Mills & Boon® book by offering you the chance to take FOUR more specially selected titles from the Modern Romance™ series absolutely FREE! We're also making this offer to introduce you to the benefits of the Reader Service™—

- ★ **FREE home delivery**
- ★ **FREE gifts and competitions**
- ★ **FREE monthly Newsletter**
- ★ **Exclusive Reader Service offers**
- ★ **Books available before they're in the shops**

Accepting these FREE books and gift places you under no obligation to buy, you may cancel at any time, even after receiving your free shipment. Simply complete your details below and return the entire page to the address below. You don't even need a stamp!

YES! Please send me 4 free Modern Romance books and a surprise gift. I understand that unless you hear from me, I will receive 6 superb new titles every month for just £2.75 each, postage and packing free. I am under no obligation to purchase any books and may cancel my subscription at any time. The free books and gift will be mine to keep in any case.

P5ZED

Ms/Mrs/Miss/Mr .... Initials ....

BLOCK CAPITALS PLEASE

Surname ....

Address ....

....

.... Postcode ....

Send this whole page to:
UK: FREEPOST CN8I, Croydon, CR9 3WZ